L

Fanged After Forty

Book 4

A Life After Magic Mystery

USA Today Bestselling Authors
Lia Davis and L.A. Boruff

Bonded in the Midlife

© Copyright 2022 Lia Davis & L.A. Boruff

Published by The Phantom Pen

PO Box 224

Middleburg, FL 32050

DavisRaynesPublishing.com

Cover by Glowing Moon Designs

Formatting by The Phantom Pen

All rights reserved under the International and Pan-American Copyright Conventions. No part of this book may be reproduced or transmitted in any form or by any means, electronic or mechanical, including photocopying, recording, or by any information storage and retrieval system, without permission in writing from the publisher.

This is a work of fiction. Names, places, characters and incidents are either the product of the author's imagination or are used fictitiously, and any resemblance to any actual persons, living or dead, organizations, events or locales is entirely coincidental.

Warning: the unauthorized reproduction or distribution of this copyrighted work is illegal. Criminal copyright infringement, including infringement without monetary gain, is investigated by the FBI and is punishable by up to 5 years in prison and a fine of $250,000.

BONDED IN THE MIDLIFE
FANGED AFTER FORTY BOOK 4

Hailey Whitfield is fed up with being told what to do, when to do it, and how she should be going about it.

Don't tell her how to live her life.

It's time for Hailey to stand up and do what needs to be done. First up, saving her brother, if he can be saved. Next, complete the mating bond with Jax, the US vampire leader. After that, who knows? Maybe she'll take on the world. Or at least the vampire council.

While she figures out what she's going to do next, Hailey's bond recovery agency, The Bond Girls, is thrown into a skip-trace that pulls at the heartstrings. What are the ladies supposed to do when the skip is being unfairly targeted?

They do what's right, of course. Too bad it's not so cut and dry. But Hailey is determined now. She's the master of her destiny, and she'll figure this out, too.

CHAPTER ONE

My brother, the darling of my life, a diva in his own right, and one of the most important people in my world, was shot four weeks ago. Four long, torturous weeks. I'd been right here every waking hour, not wanting to leave his side.

Since the shooting, which was *the* worst day of my life, he'd been comatose. Unable to move, unable to breathe on his own. As far as we knew, his mind could be barely more than mush.

According to the host of doctors working on his case, the chances of Luke ever waking were slim to none. They'd run test after test, taken blood, mapped his mind, and every other imaginable procedure, and still come up with the same conclusion—there wasn't much they could do. They'd long ago abandoned his fate to the power of prayer. They'd given up hope for his recovery.

My heart hadn't beat since the night he'd been shot. I mean, it literally didn't beat, ever, since I'm a vampire, but you know what I mean.

I wasn't giving up on him. Ever.

Those doctors, while they were at the top of their respective fields, didn't know the resilience in my family. The sturdy foundation on which we were built. Also, they didn't know I was a vampire who could breathe life into my brother. Well, drip blood, but that gets a little graphic... soooo, yeah. They had no idea.

I'd sat with Luke every day, rather every night, since days meant sunlight and sunlight meant burned to a crisp Hailey, and I'd grown rather accustomed to being *un*crispy. Something I'd never had to worry about. Only recently, actually. Not until I'd been turned into a vampire. Insert hissing sound here.

Now, sunlight was a worry. Not something to send me into a panic. I could wear long sleeves and a hat and some major layers of sunscreen.

However, the sunlight wasn't my only worry at the moment. Definitely, number one was my almost-dead brother, Luke. Then there was a council of elder vampires who had required my existence to be justified. Also, the mating bond with the smoking hot neighbor who'd turned me. And even though he was a gorgeous neighbor, being forced to form a mating bond within the time frame the elders demanded was pushing way too many of my defiant buttons. I couldn't help but think that there was an ulterior motive on their part.

This girl was wavering, though. Not because the elders said I had to mate, but because the said potential mate, Jax was worming his way into my heart. It helped that he was *hot*. You know, in case you didn't hear me the first time. He was sizzling, smoking, and a bunch more synonyms that basically meant melt my panties off.

And my thoughts were rambling, again. A product of my mind trying to keep me sane while my brother was dying.

Back to reality and my near-constant panic. I took a breath, not that I needed to breathe, but I needed to do *something*. The hospital smelled like antiseptic and illness, the two things Luke hated most in the world. Another sob stuck in my throat as I reached out to take his hand again.

Having him laid up in a bed too big for him while he looked...*less* than normal was not going to be the last memory I had of him. He would never forgive me. I'd never forgive myself. It didn't matter, ultimately, what the council said about turning Luke. I was doing it, and all the vampires in our crew suspected it. It was just a question of when and where.

I needed to make sure Jax was on board with it. To see if he'd have my back. The real test of a true mate.

Luke was gonna be mad as hell that I hadn't called Jamie—the hairdresser who maintained the razor-sharp part Luke loved in his hair—to handle the overgrowth of his face and coif.

"Don't worry, brother," I whispered, swiping a few strands of hair from his forehead. I would see to it the moment he was out of here. And that was going to be sooner than anyone else could predict. Only I knew what I'd decided about when to do it.

Jax walked in and stood beside my chair. Not only was he tall enough to cast a shadow, but there weren't many places he could go that I wouldn't know.

We were connected as maker and progeny, as to-be-bonded mates. I couldn't even think about the mating bond while Luke was ill. Not any more than I did when my mind wandered. Actually doing it was on hold until my brother was awake and well again.

But if I *was* thinking about it, I wanted to believe I wasn't so shallow as to have my decision affected by Jax's blondish hair that was a half-inch too long, or the smoldering gaze, or the body that made my mouth water. I wanted to believe I would choose to complete the ritual that would bond us as mates forever because he was kind, cared about me and my family, and the disheartening effect of my brother's near-death-ness.

"How is he?" Have I mentioned the voice? It was like a body-shiver bonus on top of the good looks.

I sighed, because, despite the involuntary trembling, there was sadness weighing me way down. "He's the same. Minimal brain activity." It hurt in my stomach to say those words. What if turning him didn't bring his brain activity back?

"That's an improvement, right?" His silky voice sounded hopeful. I hated to disappoint him.

Technically, it was. Minimal was a step up from none. Dr. Brain Scan had emphasized the word *minimal* and had said that if we were going to see real improvement, we would've seen it already. "The doctor is recommending we remove"—the words tasted bitter—"life support."

"Oh, Hailey." His hand dropped on my shoulder, but I didn't want his pity. I wanted my brother to wake up, to throw his arms out, shimmy his shoulders and call me a ridiculous bi-otch for blubbering, which I hadn't realized I was doing until Jax crouched in front of me and pulled me into a hug.

I couldn't let him hug me. When he tried to comfort me, it felt like I was going to break down even more. Like I might come apart and there'd never be another way to get me back together.

"What do Ollie and your sisters say?" Jax asked after another attempt to comfort me.

I sure as hell couldn't bother my parents with this, whether or not to take their sweet Lukey off of life support, because they wouldn't survive having to make such a decision. They'd taken a hotel room nearby and had taken turns staying here with Luke. Twenty-four-seven. I'd had to compel the doctor to tell his staff not to tell them anything.

My older brother Ollie, on the other hand, would expect to be consulted, and would expect a full dissertation that I wasn't even slightly prepared to give. There was no point in discussing anything since I knew what I was going to do.

The twins, my parents' late-in-life gifts to themselves and the youngest of our group, wouldn't be able to stop crying long enough to make a decision.

Luke was the pin that held our family together. Luke was everyone's favorite and nobody minded in the least because he was *everyone's* favorite.

I'd already sent the girls back to their Broadway rehearsals. They hadn't wanted to leave, but we talked them into it, promising to call the moment there was any news. I might have put a tiny thought that Luke would be okay. Because he would. One way or another.

It was me and Ollie. We'd be the ones to make any decisions, or at least it would be if I planned to follow the human doctors' orders. "Ollie is determined that Luke would choose to have time to heal," Jax said.

I was inclined to agree, but Dr. Pull-the-Plug hadn't been enthused by our faith in Luke's ability to recover.

There was no way we could talk in here because I didn't want Luke to overhear if that was possible. "C'mere." I pulled Jax out of Luke's room and led him to an unoccupied room down the hall.

He walked in behind me and shut the door, then smiled like I had just agreed to consummate the mating bond, or at least meant to have a tryst here in the hospital.

The snort that escaped my mouth was totally unintentional. "Down boy. We need to talk about my brother."

Sucking in a shuddering breath, I weighed my words carefully. I didn't know who Jax had brought with him or whether or not anyone from the vampire council was within earshot.

They had a habit of turning up when I least expected it and at the most inopportune times. Right now, what I had to say was not meant for their possible superhero auditory abilities. This was private. Plus, it was against vampire law and could result in my immediate termination.

"I have to turn him, Jax," I whispered so only he could hear me.

He cocked a brow. Was that disapproval on his face? I couldn't understand his resistance after what he'd done for me, turning me, a virtual stranger.

I was only asking to do the same thing for someone I'd loved literally for my entire life. "I can't..." My voice broke. The words wouldn't come. They were too hard, the thought too heartbreaking.

"Hailey—"

I held up a hand and shook my head, swallowing the tears of panic and pain. No way was I listening to him tell me it was against the rules. His suddenly being all about the vampire edicts seemed a bit over the top. "No, Jax. This is *Luke*."

He nodded his head rapidly and grabbed my arms. "Yes! And he's been valuable to the council." It was a stretch, but I appreciated the effort. "If we ask, they'll give permission. I'm sure we can convince them."

I didn't share his confidence in a council that wanted me either dead or forced into mating bond servitude—it wasn't truly as bad as all that, but I had a point to make—and I wasn't allowing them to use my brother to force my compliance. "Luke is running out of time."

The council wasn't the swiftest in their decision-making process. I didn't have that kind of patience. We should've asked them the moment he was shot. We should've sent an envoy.

Jax looked at me with eyes full of worry and pain. He was feeling my agony on top of his own. He was fond of my brother as well. "Hailey, I don't want to take on the council, yet. I don't think we'd win. Not now."

Yet was such an intriguing and promising word. It gave me a spark of hope. It was not at all applicable in this situation. I wasn't asking him to take on anyone. Also, rebelling against the council wasn't something I had time to dissect right now. I filed it away for later. "Luke doesn't have time for them to weigh his case for the pros and cons of creating a diva vampire."

Among all the other reasons, I couldn't take the chance they would go against him either. If they said no and I turned him anyway—and I would—it would be even worse than not asking for permission.

Jax squeezed my arms. "He needs more time to heal, Hailey."

Normally, the way he said my name gave me tingles, warmth where warmth *used* to be, but saving Luke was too important to set my hormones free. "He's out of time Jax. They're going to take his life support away." The doctors were pushing hard. I didn't know how long I could compel them not to do it. And what if their higher-ups got involved? We couldn't mind wash every doctor in the hospital… err, could we?

"Let's at least get Dominic on board." Dominic was Jax's maker, a council member, and our best chance if we were going to help Luke through the appropriate channels.

His look-before-we-leap attitude was not one to be reckoned with on a normal day, but today wasn't that day. Tomorrow wasn't looking good either.

"No." I shook my head decisively. "I'm doing it. Period. And I don't care about the council or their rules." Jax and I would deal with it or not, but no way was I letting Luke die. "You're either in or you're out."

I sounded like one of those baddies in the old movies Cleo loved, but few things in my life had ever been so important to me, and I wasn't waiting around for further argument. This was the end of the line.

Softening my face, I cupped Jax's cheek. "I'm sorry," I whispered. "I wish I could see another option."

Whirling, and without so much as a backward glance, I walked out into the hallway and toward my brother's room. As I approached, the door swung open and Ransom, Jax's right hand and my brother's new boy toy, walked out, wiping his mouth on a napkin. He was another who'd been here at the hospital pretty much every waking moment. Luke always had a room full of people who loved him dearly.

Ransom was about to pass me without so much as looking up. He seemed tense, almost jumpy. But there were more emotions knotted up inside him that I couldn't pinpoint what it was.

I laid a hand flat on his chest, prepared to go full-body tackle if necessary, though Ransom could soundly kick my ass. "What happened? What's wrong?" The words tumbled out of me. "Is Luke okay?"

He shrugged. Ransom was another of those pretty vamps—dark hair, gray eyes, full lips, broad shoulders, tapered waist. Luke didn't just *like* him. Luke was enchanted and Ransom, quietly as he did it, had been at Luke's side since the shooting. As much as the wide windows in Luke's room allowed.

He glanced at me. "I solved the problem you and Jax were arguing about." He nodded toward the room. "He's changing right now."

Oh, my. We weren't talking about clothes.

"So we need to get him home before the doctors try testing him."

The real power in being a vampire was in secrecy and in the way vamps could cover their tracks. Nobody truly knew we existed. No humans, anyway, and even most of the supernatural world thought we were extinct.

I wanted to be angry because Luke belonged to me. I was the resident vamp in the family, and I should've been the one who turned him, but I also couldn't blame Ransom. His feelings for Luke were obvious. So, instead of anger, I chose gratitude. He'd saved Luke and that was enough for me. And it had taken the decision off my shoulders.

For better or worse, it was done.

CHAPTER TWO

Dr. Brain VonScan was on duty tonight. He seemed to volunteer for night shifts. And in typical my luck fashion, he turned the corner and walked toward Luke's room. I sucked in a panicked breath. We couldn't let anyone near Luke until he was further along in the change process. We'd gotten lucky that my parents and Ollie weren't here at the moment, now this. Crap.

I looked at Jax, and Jax looked at me, both of us wide-eyed. Welcome to today's *oh-frick!* moment brought to us by Dr. B's bad timing.

Compel him.

One of the benefits of Jax as my maker was my ability to hear his voice in my head. It didn't sound as sexy as the real thing, but it came in a very close second, and it allowed us to communicate outside the hearing of others. And he didn't live rent-free in my head or anything, just when he needed to tell me something. And it seemed to only work one way. I couldn't project my thoughts to him. That was his vampire gift, not mine.

My compel-the-human game needed work, and this probably wasn't the best time to flex that muscle, what with the urgency of the situation. One of us had to act fast. Dr. B was closing in, and Jax had put it in my hands. Erm, my head. Dang it.

I focused my energy on his stethoscope because sometimes a single object helped. In my head I chanted, "Remove."

Jax said short commands worked best, and I wanted to start small. My goal was to get the good doctor to take the stethoscope from around his neck and put it in his pocket.

Start small then aim big.

Jax's words.

He'd also said that to compel a person to act took practice, and I might've skimped a bit on that part. Honestly, who liked doing things they weren't good at? More than that, I'd been at the hospital pretty much every moment I wasn't eating or sleeping. Maybe I should've been practicing by compelling the hospital staff, but that just felt icky.

Oh, man. I really should've practiced on *someone*. Dr. B took off his stethoscope all right, and when that was in his pocket, he shrugged off his lab coat.

I gaped at the man as he loosened his tie, then when he flicked open the button on his slacks, I held up a hand in the universal motion for *stop*.

Oh, no. Down went the pants. Holding my hand out accomplished very little except to hide his dangling pecker.

"Please stop," I whispered, desperately trying to compel him to put his clothes back on, but he continued unbuttoning his dress shirt as he kicked off his shoes then stepped out of his puddled slacks.

Things had taken a very sharp left turn. Jax was going to have to step in.

At the thought of Jax and my failure, I entirely gave up trying to compel the nearly naked doctor and looked at my maker.

Jax wore a gigantic smile, just this side of outright laughter. Whether it was regarding my lack of skill or the doctor's exposure, it wasn't helpful.

I needed this doctor, who it turned out was *highly* suggestible, to say that Luke was healed, that he was a medical marvel, nay, a *miracle*. And no way would he say it without someone in his head helping him figure it out. Even if I managed to get him to say it, no one was going to believe him if he didn't put his tallywacker away.

I looked at Jax, but he shook his head. As I gaped at him in shock, Jax waved me on. "Fix it."

The doc had come to himself when I stopped trying. He yanked up his pants, looking around, probably asking himself why in the world he'd done that. Poor guy.

Sucking in a deep breath I tried again and this time, dear old Dr. Brain blinked slowly.

Dress yourself.

Slowly, so slowly I wanted to gouge my own eyes out, the man reassembled all his clothing, buttoning his buttons and tying his tie. Then, the doctor walked toward Luke's room with me beside him. Proximity and focus were the keys to compulsion. I stayed close, with my gaze glued to the physician.

He's healed.

The doc blinked a few times, then grabbed a tablet off the side table. Probably left by a nurse. This hospital did everything via tablet or laptop. Very high tech. No paper charts here.

It's a miracle. Look how perfect he is. Like he was never shot.

"I can't believe how this patient recovered," he mumbled. "I've never seen anything like it."

Update his record. Luke wants to go home right away, now that he's awake and back to normal.

Jax had said keep it simple, so I switched to chanting, *Send Luke home. Send Luke home.*

I watched over the good doctor's shoulder as he typed on the tablet, proclaiming my brother a bona fide medical mystery, and scribbled his name at the bottom of the screen.

Go on a long break. Go on a long break.

Dr. BrainScan rubbed his eyes. "I need a coffee. Congratulations on Luke's recovery."

"Great job," Jax said, beaming at me as he helped Ransom unlock the brakes on the bed.

Ransom went ahead as a lookout while Jax and I pushed it out the door.

In fairness and in defense of the makers of the Air-O-Matic adjustable hospital bed, they probably weren't meant to adapt to vampire speed and as Jax rounded a corner, pushing the bed, one of the wheels jerked off and flew to the left, punching a hole in the drywall. The bed tilted and Luke rolled.

Lurching forward, I caught him before he hit the ground. Crouched beside the bed, I looked around and tried not to panic. There was no way someone wasn't going to show up any second now. It was about to be a dang compulsion festival in here.

Jax took Luke from me. "Better if someone sees me carrying him rather than you."

Good point. It was no big deal, not with my vampire strength, for me to cart him all over the place, but it would look awfully odd.

Ransom peered around the corner seconds later, then disappeared before jogging into sight with a wheelchair. "Thank goodness," I muttered.

We left the bed against the wall, hopefully covering the hole because, while Ransom would have disabled the security cameras, folks were milling around. We'd gotten beyond lucky to have this corridor empty at the moment.

Luke tilted in the chair and Ransom held onto him with one hand on Luke's shoulder and the other pushing the chair. By the time we made it to the car, Luke was half-awake but still glassy-eyed and only partially changed. It would take time. I slept through most of mine, but I hadn't been jostled around a hospital in the process.

Dawn was coming and we needed to be home with Luke inside before the sun came up. Jax drove as fast as he could without drawing attention to our vehicle. Even taking the time to compel a cop was too much time right now.

When we pulled up at Jax's place, I looked at Ransom. "Just let me run across the street and get the door open. Then you can carry him over." I eyed the space between Jax's driveway and mine. "Maybe you could pull the car over there so there's less time for someone to see Luke being carried in."

Ransom frowned. "I thought he would stay with me." He nodded to Jax's place and that made sense because Ransom was Luke's maker…except that Luke was my brother.

Their relationship was too new. Luke wouldn't want Ransom to see him without his hours of prep. They were still in the stage for Luke to always be the well-coiffed, gorgeous man he presented to the world, and most especially to the man he was interested in.

Knowing everything Ransom had seen over the last few weeks would kill Luke, and we'd already talked about keeping it our secret. Ransom wouldn't tell.

I sighed. This wasn't a fight I wanted to have with the poor guy. I had to think about Luke and what he would want. Luke was my brother. He belonged with me.

There was only one way to solve this. "You can stay at my place, too." Safety in numbers and all that.

Ransom nodded broadly. "That works."

Dawn was peeking over the horizon, and I was still wide awake, which was an oddity. Did vampires get adrenaline rushes? This felt like an adrenaline rush. Normally, by this time of day, I was tired and tucked, halfway into a dream about Jax.

As soon as I was in my house, fatigue hit, and it was all I could do to muster the energy to get a room ready for Ransom and Luke. I fought the yawns until Luke was settled and then went to my room, flopped on my bed, and passed out.

I slept like a rock and woke up just before dusk. Luke wouldn't be awake until after dark had fully fallen if he even woke today. I lounged in my bed and crafted a to-do list comprised of about a thousand phone calls, a couple of hundred explanations, and chores that would make living with Luke less drama, more simpatico. He needed his *things*. All the things. And he'd never forgive me if I forced him to use my three-year-old bottle of Aqua Net instead of his Oribe line of hair products. Or whatever higher-end brand he was into at the moment.

I had to call my parents, Ollie, the twins, the gallery he ran. They all needed to be made aware of Luke's *miraculous* recovery. That was what I had in mind to call it, anyway. Although seeing Luke with blood-hunger shining red in his eyes and new feral darkness might stretch *miraculous* and *recovery* beyond their definitions.

Letting Luke die had been out of the question. Period. So, for that, I was beyond grateful to Ransom. And I always would be, but also still slightly irritated because Luke had been my hero since I was a child. He'd been a boy, and then a man unafraid of being who he was. This had been my one chance to be his hero.

Too late now. The council meeting was held virtually, as usual, with everyone calling in on their laptops or phones. Pearl sat at the edge of Jax's desk, just out of sight of the camera, but able to see and hear everything. Jax and I had warned the rest of the council she probably would. They were eager to partner with the hunters as well and not have them coming after vampires all the time, potentially the world over.

The hunters had been active before the vampires had pulled off the ultimate fake death and got the world believing all of the vampires were extinct. Before the hunters had believed they'd eradicated all bloodsuckers from the planet, they'd forced all of us into deep hiding. Living openly the way we had been in Philadelphia hadn't been possible.

Now that they knew we existed again, we had no choice but to prove our civility.

We discussed a few vampire change propositions, how the hunt for rogues was going, and we argued about the new rules.

Now I just had to figure out how to deal with Ollie. He'd seen Luke lying in bed, barely clinging to life. The others did too, but as the oldest son, Ollie was more observant and the one to take charge most of the time. And thanks to the posse of brain doctors who'd been so diligent in their updates, he'd heard that Luke was a lost cause. Certainly, he would have doubts that it would work. Miracles weren't something Ollie believed in. Or trusted. And where Ollie had doubts, he liked to share them until everyone in his vicinity had them, too.

I didn't have the heart to use my voice to lie to him or allow him to grill me on it, so I shot him a text. Definitely the coward's way out.

Doctors said they've never seen such a miraculous recovery as Luke's. I've brought him home.

I added a smiley face and a red heart then hit send. The shit was about to hit the fan.

The text was enough to inspire action, and before I was off the phone with my parents, who I called the moment after I sent the text, and who I'd downplayed the total of Luke's injuries the whole time, Ollie was at my front door.

Ransom let him in, and Ollie didn't even look at me as he brushed past to stand in front of Luke, who we'd nestled on the sofa, and stare down at him. Luke smiled, although he had yet to speak since he'd woken. I'd gotten that much from Ransom while talking to my folks.

Ollie was wearing his big brother attitude with an added dose of indignation. "Why didn't you call me?" The question was meant for me, but he hadn't stopped staring at Luke.

He knew what I was, which meant he knew what I did the instant he read my text.

I wasn't any more impressed with Ollie now than I'd been when we were teenagers when he tried this crap. Like him being the big brother made us his responsibility. Maybe when we were very small, but come on. We're all adults.

He moved closer to Luke, pulled our younger brother's upper lip up as if he was looking for fangs, but what big brother didn't realize was that Luke's fangs wouldn't pop until it was time to eat.

Before I finished the thought, I heard the tell-tale pop of Luke's fangs descending. Uh oh. Being human, with human auditory abilities, Ollie had no idea what was happening, and Luke pounced. He sank his teeth into Ollie's forearm.

Oops.

For only a second, chaos ensued. Ollie screamed and tried yanking his arm away, but Luke had a strong grip. Too bad Ollie couldn't just chill a minute and let Ransom and me figure it out, but no. Ollie pulled back, lifting Luke from the sofa and dragging him around, knocking the flower arrangement–fake as it was–from the coffee table and onto the floor where the vase shattered. Ransom righted the TV when Ollie backed into it and tilted it askew on its hanging arm. Jax saved the day when he burst through the front door and went straight for Luke, prying his mouth off of Ollie's arm and pushing Luke to the sofa.

Had this not been a Moment—with a capital M—I was having, I would have taken the time to stare at Jax. The man was powerful. And power on that fella was enough to make my heart race.

But I was up to my backside in brothers. One was hungry and wiping his mouth as he stared at Ollie like he was a filet mignon, and the other was angry. Furious. This wasn't going to look good in the family newsletter.

Luke advanced again, this time, his hands like claws, and I wondered if he wasn't confusing vampire-ness with that werewolf movie we'd watched when we were kids.

Jax looked at Ransom. "Control him."

Ransom yanked Luke away from Ollie, who shot me a glare so angry I should've melted under the weight of it, but I crossed my arms and stared back.

"Why the hell did you do this to Luke?" he growled. "Surely there was time to let him heal."

This was an if-looks-could-kill situation and had Ollie not been my brother, I would've displayed for him what vampire anger could do the job his piddly human look couldn't. But he was my brother, and this situation wasn't one any of us had experience with.

"No," I said flatly. "There was no more time."

Still, I couldn't resist a little teasing. I faked shame and ducked my head. "When I first turned, I took a nibble out of Luke." I watched him from beneath my lashes. His eyes went wide as I continued. "And now Luke has taken a nibble of you." I let my grin spread. "Maybe you're next!"

The fake excitement was a little over-acted, but Ollie stared, wide-eyed at the bite mark on his arm. "You'd better be joking." Poor guy. His voice sounded like I'd knocked all the wind out of his sails.

"Of course I am." I sighed. Ollie never could take a joke. Could hardly tell when someone was joking. Maybe it was the price of being the oldest. Maybe not. "He was going to die, Ollie."

"So now he's a freak?" He glared at me with his lip curled.

What? All my playful attempts to calm Ollie faded and I glared at him. "Four *freaks* to one angry brother. I like our odds."

I jerked a thumb toward the vampires in the room, and Ollie backed up as I flashed my sweetest smile. I'd compel him if I had to, or at least try, but it would make me a lot happier if he'd just accept it and move on.

He looked from Luke to me and back to Luke. It was odd for Luke to be so quiet, but he wasn't quite grown into his vampire-hood, and I was grateful his sassy mouth wasn't interrupting. Ollie hated the full-on diva-tude Luke usually greeted him with. He was the buttoned-up brother, and he approved of so little that Luke and I did, nine times out of ten, we lied to him to save ourselves the older-bro lecture.

Thankfully, though, Luke was too busy admiring his fangs in the reflection of my blackened TV screen.

Ollie sighed. "Whatever." He laid a hand on Luke's shoulder, grimaced, then quickly drew it back. Probably he remembered the bite mark on the other arm and didn't want to take another chance. "I'm glad you're alive...sort of." He must've heard how it sounded because he shook his head. "Fully glad, sort of alive, I mean."

Luke nodded. "You taste like peanut butter." Then he scraped his tongue over his teeth, his face part sneer, part grimace. Luke hated peanut butter.

Ransom turned Luke toward the kitchen. "Blood types all have their own taste. As well as people. You'll get used to it." As they walked away, Ransom continued explaining. "There are variables."

I tuned them out and focused on Ollie. "You're explaining this one to Mom."

He snorted. "Not likely."

"You need to think of something because they will be here within the hour. You need to convince them that Luke is getting better, and they should return home." I toed the edge of the couch and refused to meet my big brother's judgmental stare.

"Oh no, Hailey. This is your mess." Ollie pursed his lips at me. I didn't even have to look at him to know he was giving me his biggest brother look.

"Well, they'll be here in about an hour, and you can't leave until they do. You're the oldest. If they see you agree with me, then they'll feel better about returning home." I tried to give him my best pouty face, but that had never worked on Ollie.

We stared at each other for a few seconds until he looked away first. "Fine, I'll stay and help you. I don't think Dad's heart could take the news that two of his five kids are vampires."

True. I was surprised they'd made the trip to Philly, but then again if my child was dying nothing would keep me from seeing him.

I moved to the kitchen to check on Luke. He was leaning against the counter with a bag of blood stuck to his fangs. The color in his cheeks was brighter, but that was thanks to the blood and only temporary.

When he met my gaze, I said, "Mom and Dad will be stopping by in a few. That means you need a crash course on not biting the humans."

He frowned and tried to talk around the bag, making a mess down his chin and shirt. Seeing all that blood made my fangs lower. In all the chaos since Ollie got here, I'd forgotten to have my breakfast. I was still a fairly newb vamp myself.

That was something I needed remedy before the folks got here.

I WAS FED. Luke was fed. Jax said he could wait. He was old enough that he didn't have to eat as often as Luke, and I needed to. Ransom was the same, although, I was pretty sure he wasn't as old as Jax.

Anyhow, we were ready for my parents, who were usually early for everything.

On that note, my doorbell rang. Luke sprang to his feet and fanned his face. "I can't do this." Then he ran down the hall.

At least he was feeling a bit more like himself. The fanged diva.

I was torn between answering the door or going after Luke and dragging his behind back into the living room. Jax stepped up beside me, but it was Ollie who spoke as he pushed in front of me to answer the door. "Go get Luke. I'll let them in."

I rushed down the hallway to the room Luke was staying in. "Luke," I whispered as I entered the room. I remembered my first night as a vampire. My senses had been heightened and way too sensitive. "Mom and Dad won't go back home unless they're sure you are healing."

He sat on his bed with his back to the headboard and knees pressed to his chest. "What if I bite them, Hails? I'd never forgive myself."

I sat on the bed, facing him. "You bit Ollie and he's fine."

"Ollie deserved to be bit," he grumbled.

I snorted. "Yeah. True." I waited for another second, listening to our parents' voices as they talked with Ollie, and he introduced them to Jax and Ransom.

"Did Ollie just tell them that Jax is my fiancé?" I asked, aghast.

Luke fell over on the bed laughing. "He did." Then he stood. "Okay. The laugh was what I needed. I'm ready now."

I eyed him. "That was fast."

Luke winked. "They'll be so distracted with your new fiancé, they won't process that I look brighter eyed and paler than I should."

Rolling my eyes, I stood. "Remember, you just got shot and made a *miraculous* recovery, you still need to *look* like you are recovering."

He waved me off as he slowed his pace and practiced his death walk to the living room. More like a zombie walk. This was not going to go well.

Together, Luke and I emerged from the hallway, and our mother rushed over to hug us. She took extra care with Luke like he would break if she squeezed too hard. When she pulled back, she studied both of us. I worried she would somehow know we were different.

"Luke, you look pale. Have you eaten?" Mom asked.

I spoke up with a little squeak in my voice. "Yes. I fixed your famous chicken noodle soup for him earlier. He's pale because he's recovering from a gunshot wound."

Man, I hated lying to my parents. But it was better than announcing we were vamps. I turned just as my dad wrapped me in a hug. "I'm disappointed that you haven't told us about Jaxon here."

I sent my beau a smile. He grinned back, obviously liking that Ollie called him my fiancé. Figures. "Well, Dad, a lot has gone on. My focus has been on Luke and making sure he got better."

Mom pulled away from Luke and eyed me. "Hailey, really. A wedding? *Again?*"

Just then, Kendra entered the house, sparing me from laying down the law with my mother. She didn't bother knocking because I'd have just told her to come in anyway. She was like family to me.

My parents' faces lit up when they saw her. Mom rushed over and hugged her. "You look good," she gushed.

I frowned. I got, "*Again?*" and Kendra got, "You look good." Figures. She was always their favorite, and she wasn't even their daughter. I was so telling the twins when I talked to them next.

However, I was thrilled that my bestie was there. She knew exactly what to do to keep them from asking too many questions. Now that I thought about it, there was most likely magic involved in that particular talent of hers.

Speaking of which, it was time for me to do my own little magic. Alter the memories of my parents. To let them believe they spent a few hours with him and that he was out of the woods. On the road to recovery.

For the next hour, I focused on the sneakiest and subtlest compulsions I'd done to date.

When Mom and Dad left, Ollie did as well. And boy was I ready for a nap. The last month had been way too stressful for this vampire.

CHAPTER THREE

June 2

Luke stood in the kitchen doorway looking at me, then away, then back at me. "I could hear you talking to me." Never before had he looked so like he was about to start crying. "The whole time. I heard you."

His soft voice danced across the room, tickling my ears and driving straight to my soul a warm balm. A tonic. The relief was potent, and tears pooled in my eyes. "I knew you could." I hadn't known squat, but I'd hoped. And I'd kept talking.

Luke shrugged and kicked the toe of his shoe against my linoleum floor. "I could've gone the rest of my life without hearing that story about you and JJ Summers on prom night." He faked a shudder.

I flushed. I probably could've chosen less of a Dear Diary moment to share with him. "Sorry. I thought maybe I could shock you awake." My voice caught as the first of the tears fell.

"Ollie gone?" He took my hand and held it.

I nodded and fought against sobs. "I'm sure he'll be back."

"Well, I need to thank you all." He took a second to give me, Jax, and Ransom each a solemn look. "You could've given up on me and you didn't. That means a lot."

I wanted to cup his face and tell him I'd always be here for him, but I might not always be. Instead, I sniffled and squeezed his hand. "Says as much about you as it does about us." I swiped my nose, then he pulled me against him into a long, strong hug I'd thought I would never feel again. The idea inspired more sobs, more tears, and more gratitude. When I could speak, I said, "I think things went well with Mom and Dad."

He chuckled and kissed the top of my head. I could sense that he wasn't quite ready to let me go yet. I was more than okay with that. "A little magic and compulsion helped."

Luke was Mom's favorite, next to Kendra. Even more so than the twins who were the babies of the family, and the last few weeks had almost killed her and Dad.

After a few more minutes I pulled back to study my brother. For a guy whose eyes said he was suffering a big bad case of blood lust, he was remarkably restrained. The only sign of his discomfort was his red eyes. He was his calm, cool self. Pre-out Luke, but Luke.

I shifted my attention to Jax. Sometimes I couldn't believe I was so connected to him. He was gorgeous. Tall but not so much I strained my neck looking up at him. Blond but not so light I needed sunglasses to be in a room with him. Muscular but not a bodybuilder. Jax Parsons wasn't the kind of too much that said trying too hard. He was exactly perfect. And sometimes, I found it intimidating.

This wasn't one of those times.

I wasn't falling all over myself to complete the edict of the council that we complete the mating bond ritual. I was coming around to the idea. The more time I spent with Jax, and especially with how he'd helped me with Luke, staying near me night and day, making sure I had everything I needed. He'd been an absolute dream.

Well, it wasn't like I had a choice. And stalling was only putting off the inevitable. Though the thought of completing the bond while Luke had been laid up had been repugnant.

That same near perfection of Jax's was one of the reasons I wasn't embracing the bond. It was a lot for a girl to live up to. We felt unequally yoked, in some ways.

He smiled at me, and I did the teenage-girl sigh. I couldn't help it. The mating bond was always at the forefront of my mind and on my to-do list. Only pushed aside by worries about Luke. Well, deciding on it, anyway. When Jax was close, I leaned more toward accepting. Actually, more toward insisting. There was no doubt that I would mate with him. What was I waiting for, besides pissing off the council?

Luke sent a text to Dad since Mom didn't have a cell phone. The two of them were always together so she didn't see the need to have one. Luke put his phone back into his pocket. "I told them to call when they land so we know they made it home okay."

I nodded as Ransom stepped in front of Luke, pulling him close. This was the most PDA they'd ever shown, so when Ransom tilted Luke's chin up and lowered his head, Jax leaned into me. "We should give them a few minutes."

In all honesty, I didn't want to get too far from Luke. I couldn't stand the thought of how close I'd come to losing him. The idea was more than I could deal with. But my brother smiled at Ransom, the guy who'd saved him, and it was a bit easier to walk away. He was in good hands.

For the first time, I saw the love between them. That gave me hope that everything would be okay. In fact, I think this was the longest Luke had been exclusive with anyone.

I headed to the front porch with Jax. We sat in silence for a few seconds as I stared at his house across the street, in wonder at my good luck at having come across this place and these people when I'd moved out here.

Jax stood next to me, smelling good, and I inhaled because resisting urges like that seemed silly. Unreasonable, even. We were alone on the porch, Luke healthy and undead inside. What reason did I have to resist any urge when it came to Jax?

The object of my affection—obsession? No, not quite that. Just affection—turned and pointed all that potent masculinity in my direction.

Hello.

I could've swooned and it wouldn't have been overacting. But I remained upright.

Barely.

"Now that Luke is back on his feet…" When he spoke in that lower, sexier register of his voice, my body hummed. Purred. Throbbed with wanting him.

Over the last few weeks, while Luke was sick, we'd hashed over the mating bond, going over every aspect of it. I was running out of resistance. To be honest, my resistance was thin enough to be almost nonexistent. I was pretty much ready to go through with it.

Commitment was my biggest weakness, my strongest insecurity. It had taken months with Jax to overcome my fears.

"Yeah?" I asked.

He grinned, and I couldn't stop myself from smiling back. "You wanna?"

We didn't even need to say all the words, and not because he was my maker, and I could hear his thoughts when he projected them to me. It was because since this had started with the council's edict, neither of us could think of much else. And I did wanna, to my pleasure and it was still a bit of a surprise.

I glanced at him quickly and it wasn't enough. I needed a real look. I soaked in his expression of tender passion. His very features melted into a mask that said he truly cared about me. "Yes," I whispered.

His smile was only the beginning of my rewards. We were due some alone time, some sexy time. Bond or no bond, I wanted Jax with every fiber of my being.

Thinking of the alone time, and as badly as I wanted him, I put a hand on his arm. "But this needs to be special." I wasn't settling for a wham-bam when this bond was as forever as a relationship could get. We were vampires, so unless the hunters found us and offed us, we were immortal, and it was my understanding that *bonded* meant till death did we part. Even if that was two-thousand years from now.

"Definitely." He captured my hands in his and brought them to his lips. The kiss wasn't anything to write home to mom about, but my stomach tingled, then it morphed into a full-body tremble when he added, "Friday?" before resuming his lip-caress of my fingertips.

If not for the softness of his voice, the tenderness of his touch, and the sexiness of his smile, I might've been able to summon the gumption to suggest a date with a bit more time to plan, but all those things that made Jax who he was were working against me. Or maybe they were working *for* me. I'd be keeping him, after all.

And then he added a soft kiss and a promise. "I'll make it special."

Even if I wanted to, which I didn't, I couldn't have said no.

Who could've?

CHAPTER FOUR

Anticipation built every day this week. Like a skyscraper of nerves, reaching high in the sky. Maybe more so because he'd kept his preparations on the DL, swearing Ransom, Grim, Paige, Luke, and even Kendra to complete secrecy. I knew they were dirty-rotten-secret-keepers because I'd badgered, cajoled, even tried bribery to no avail. Their loyalty to Jax was unmatched.

Even *Kendra*! She was supposed to be loyal to me, but all she'd do all week was tap the side of her nose and wink as if I had the first dang clue what that meant.

When Friday finally came, with the speed of a snail on vacation, I stood in front of my mirror in a strapless, black, silk dress that hugged my curves and caressed my skin with every move. Luke had picked it out and I had to give it to him. It looked amazing on my vampirific body. All svelte curves and soft lines.

I'd put on enough makeup to enhance my pasty skin, but not so much that my morning after would see me with raccoon eyes or a pillow's worth of foundation. I was going for subtle and understated. Not desperate. Besides, it wasn't like I got a lot of acne or anything now. And while my complexion color left something to be desired, I was virtually poreless, which was a condition women paid thousands to achieve. Mwahahaha.

Jax headed across the street from his place, and even though I wasn't looking out the window, I knew exactly where he was. Not only his presence but his heightened emotions. He was nervous. Probably not as much as I was, but not as cool as his usual cucumber self. Hurrying down the hall, I thought about him being able to read my nervousness as well.

I couldn't always sense his emotions like this, but I'd learned to hone the ability over the last few weeks.

No doubt it would be stronger, and harder to control, once the bond was complete.

When he rang the bell, and I swung the door open, I sucked in a breath. This was a man who knew how to wear a suit. Black on black with a black tie. Sounded like a bit much, but on Jax it made my mouth water and my anticipation turned to expectation.

He was a dream. No, better. Jax was a fantasy come to life, and it wasn't the clothes or the fact that he was the best-looking man I'd ever cast a gaze at. It was the look in his eyes, the one that said he wanted me. Me! Little ol' me.

Not that men hadn't in the past wanted me, but this was more. This was electric. This was Jamie and Claire level wanting. I'll follow you across the centuries wanting. We wouldn't have to travel through stones to see two hundred years pass, though. We'd just wait for the time to pass around us.

Would I ever get tired of seeing him? Would there come a time when the electricity faded into complacency?

I couldn't imagine it happening. Not on my part.

The unknown that Jax might one day get tired of me—that was the main reason I'd been resistant. I hated not knowing.

But life couldn't give me certainty. That wasn't how this worked.

We stood in the doorway, me inside, him still on the threshold, gazing at each other. His emotions hit me harder this close together. He was as infatuated as I was. And as unsure of the future. But he was willing to take the plunge, even without knowing how I'd come to feel about him in years to come.

Instead of trying to come in, he held out his hand, and I slipped mine into his. Not having a body temperature that could be measured on a human thermometer didn't stop heat from building in my belly. It might've been residual, but I'd been a vampire for a while, so I doubted it. It was psychological, just like the feeling that my heart was racing in my chest.

It wasn't.

He smiled. I smiled. Neither of us moved. Somehow, though, it didn't feel awkward. Even with Ransom and Luke in the living room behind me. Everything felt right. Like the world was clicking into place. Finally.

"Should–should we go?" I liked that he had to clear his throat to take it down an octave. He was somehow as awestruck as I was. Damn, that felt good. To be wanted. Desired.

I grinned and walked onto the porch next to him. I wasn't a clumsy kind of girl, but I paid extra attention to my three-inch heels, so I didn't embarrass myself by landing on my face at the bottom of the stairs. Vampirism gave speed and strength, and it did aid a bit in my gracefulness, but it did *not* prevent me from having accidents. I was still susceptible to face-planting.

I'd thought we were just going to go to his house and let the mating begin—insert fanfare here—but apparently, he'd made other plans, plans that involved driving. Was this an actual date? How exciting.

A car was magically in front of my house–not his daily driver, but a very sleek, black sports car I'd seen once parked in his garage. It hadn't been there the last time I'd looked out. Perks of being the king, I supposed.

At the sidewalk, he squeezed my hand. He knew I was worried and wanted to comfort me. I felt it coming through our sire bond.

Seconds later, after he opened my door for me, we were off. Once upon a time, I might've balked at him opening my door, but not now. Now it put a smile on my face. Heck, I could've ripped the door *off* of the car if I'd given a bit of effort. It wasn't about me needing to be cared for. It was about him caring enough to open my door. A gesture.

Be still my heart.

He drove us to a park that was nearby but too far to walk to in heels. There were couples already here, sitting on blankets, everyone facing toward the stage where a band was setting up. This was such a wholesome, *normal* sort of date. How thoughtful of him to think of it.

I smiled as he spread out the blanket. It took a second as I watched the muscles of his back expand and contract under his dress shirt before I wondered how in heaven's name I was going to sit in this dress. It was snug where dresses were meant to be snug, and there was no graceful way to go from standing to sitting. Maybe if he helped me lie down prostrate on the blanket.

Bless him. He had *not* thought out this part. He should've had Kendra or Luke warn me to dress differently.

Part of the issue was the shoes, so I bent to remove them. Jax held out his arm for me to use as leverage. Nothing sexy, just sweet and kind. There went my heart, fake beating again.

I made it to the ground and hiked up my skirt to create a little bit of breathing room around my hips. It wasn't too ladylike, but I pulled up the corner of the blanket to cover myself. The dress would wrinkle, but at least I'd be able to enjoy the moment. That was all that mattered.

The band took the stage and around us people stood and clapped, so I straightened and clapped along with them. And then when the music started, Jax had eyes only for me. I gazed at him like he'd hung the moon because I was in that state of mind. With a half-smile, the corner of his mouth crooked upward, he pulled me against him, then moved back and forth with me in his arms.

He wasn't trying to Swayze me. We were just two normal people listening to the music while we rocked to and fro. At least that was what we looked like, but to me, it was so much more. It was anticipation. Desire. Longing. Necessity. An order by the council. More desire. More longing. An inevitability. This was foreplay to the foreplay that was likely to come.

It was a look, a touch, a smile.

When I was younger, I'd wanted a guy to serenade me with his guitar outside my bedroom window. I'd wanted poems and sonnets. I'd wanted the grand gesture. As I grew older, I'd realized that was all ridiculous. Real life didn't work that way. Real men didn't do that stuff. Only in movies.

But that was *before*, too. Before I met Jax. Before this moment. Before the night that was coming. Jax was so much better than real men. He was everything.

We listened to the music, swaying in place and murmuring to one another while we sat in the blanket under the big oak tree near the statue garden.

During a break in the music, we sat close, and he rubbed his hand over mine, holding them up and measuring mine against his. He traced my fingers with his. This was a man who knew how to use touch to his every advantage. "Are you nervous?"

I wasn't. Not anymore. Not now. No doubt he knew that. I knew his nerves had settled as well. "More curious," I said as I looked into his eyes.

I could've poked around in his thoughts, but I wouldn't have liked him nosing into mine, so I asked the question instead. "How does the mating bond ritual work?"

"Procedurally?" He chuckled.

"Logistically." I didn't need to know every step, but an overview would ease my remaining jitters. I hoped.

"It's simple enough." His smile softened as he brushed a stray hair off of my face and tucked it behind my ear, then let his finger drag along my jaw to my chin and then down my throat. "We'll mate."

If I was the kind of vampire whose cheeks could flush from a rush of blood, mine would've. I wasn't sure if what I was feeling was a result of wishing or if it was a residual of my humanity. It didn't matter. I had a lot of feelings to control right now. This was only one of them.

"Mate?" I whispered, my breath choked in my throat. Why was I trying to breathe? I'd forgotten I didn't need to for a moment. Did he mean sex? I really hoped so, but that was nothing new for us. We'd been doing that for a while now, albeit not often while Luke was injured.

"In the very human way." Somehow, I doubted it, but I didn't interrupt. "And while we do, we'll inject one another with our venom."

"Like...?" I pantomimed a needle injection.

He smiled and his fangs popped. "More like this." And he ran his tongue around one, then the other. I'd never seen anything so purely sexy. My panties might as well have melted off of me right then. Holy vampire sex, Batman.

"So we..." I swallowed hard. "*Bite* each other?" I could go for that.

He nodded. "Every night for a moon's cycle."

"Don't the lunar cycles belong to the lycanthropes?" I'd done some reading. Quite a bit of reading, actually. It was one of the things that had kept me sufficiently distracted so I didn't worry myself sick over Luke. And it would've been easy to convey how smart and learned I was if he wasn't massaging my hand with his.

"You always surprise me." He ducked his head and kissed my hand again, then looked up at me. "And yes. The moon cycles are lycanthropic, but we use that time as a measure. That's all. Not the actual cycle, just the number of days."

I nodded as if I understood, but he could've told me we had to go to the moon and walk around before the ritual, and because of the desire in his eyes, I wouldn't have disagreed.

For that matter, could we walk around on the moon without space suits? A question for another day.

The concert was over, and we sat together under a sky full of stars, almost alone now since the park was emptying, and he still had his hand in mine. Still had his body pressed close.

I sighed, content to never move out of the circle of his arms, but too soon, he let go and bent to pull me to my feet, then picked up the blanket. He didn't fold it but rolled it into a ball and carried it under one arm, then held my hand as we walked toward the car.

As he drove, the radio played more love songs, and Jax hummed along, stopping every once in a while, to gaze at me and smile. I smiled back, of course, because I wanted him to know that I was happy we were about to mate and bond.

When he turned onto our street, I hoped we would be heading to his place, since Luke and Ransom were at mine. He pulled the car into his garage and my body hummed along with the garage door as it slid down the rail, shutting us in.

We'd been alone in a park full of people, but now we were *alone,* alone. And I was excited. Anticipation made my hands tremble, and my knees shake until he opened my door and helped me out.

There was something decadent, almost, about knowing what was going to happen. This wasn't just sex. This was a promise. I ran my fingers down the inside of his arm as we made our way around the car to the steps leading inside.

This was my moment. My favorite of this night so far. The excitement. The happiness. The need and expectation, the desire and suspense. It was a potent combination.

As I walked inside, he moved his hand to the small of my back and when the door shut behind us, he moved to stand in front of me. "I'm nervous, I'm not too proud to admit." I knew he was, and that helped ease my nerves.

It was arguably the most endearing thing he'd ever said to me. It certainly made me like him more than I already did, and I hadn't thought that was possible.

Instead of answering, I rose onto my tiptoes and pulled him down for a kiss. Jax had about a thousand skills, some I knew, some I didn't, but of the ones I knew, the one where he truly shone was this. The man knew how to kiss, where to put his hands, how to hold a woman so that her clothes practically fell off.

Mine did. Or somehow, without ripping them, they ended up in a pile on the floor. And we must've floated to his bedroom because too soon and not soon enough, I found myself lying in his bed, wrapped in his arm, his fangs plunged into the soft tissue between my neck and shoulder. I didn't know when his clothes had come off either but never was a woman more grateful than I for a naked man.

His bite started an orgasm that coursed through me like a pounding headache, except instead of pain, there was ecstasy.

And then I was on him, returning that favor and adding a bite just below his ear as he lifted his hips and plunged inside of me. His blood poured into my mouth, intensifying the orgasm as it continued its wild escapade through my body, heightened by every thrust of his hips.

I could've looked at him, tasted him, stayed in bed, and let him thrust into me over and over again, bit and been bitten until morning peeked through the curtain and made a triangle on the floor. But too soon, my climax waned. We rested side by side, breathing like we needed the oxygen, but more out of habit and afterglow than anything.

He turned his head and smiled. "I'm spent."

I felt his happy exhaustion through the bond. It was stronger now like it'd been renewed. Though, oddly, not as potent as I'd expected. I'd figured I'd be overwhelmed with it. This was... pleasant.

There were a thousand things in my head. Most of them were Jax, and happiness at the afterglows of the mating process, but there were a couple that weren't. Like the council. I sighed and shook my head. They'd had no right to force us into this. That experience should've been a private matter, done between Jax and me when we saw fit and not a moment sooner.

"Are you unhappy?" he asked, looking slightly crestfallen. Worry came through the bond.

Oh, no. Had I said it aloud? But then, no, I didn't have to for Jax to know what I was thinking.

Unhappy? "No!" I exclaimed.

He sat up now on one elbow and looked down at me. "Did you only do this because of the council?"

"Hell, no." My head shake was fast and fervent. He needed to know, for sure, how I felt. I'd never want him to feel unsure of me. Truth time. "I did it because I love you." How he could think otherwise was disheartening. "This was why I hesitated. I didn't want you to think I did it because they made us. I did it because I wanted to."

His smile spread across his face, and he didn't reply for a few seconds. Strong emotions, love, pounded through our bond. "Good."

I tried to explain myself a little better. "I'm only saying this should have entirely been our choice. Not an edict by them. It almost cheapens it that we didn't get the chance to do such a beautiful thing on our own." I looked him over, from where his shoulder to his hip and back up to the icy blue of his eyes. "Did you only do it because the council forced your hand?"

He ran his finger across my collarbone, the touch both gentle and sweet. "I have wanted you to be mine since the first day I met you. Since I saw you sitting on your porch with Kendra watching your movers carrying your furniture inside." That day seemed like a thousand years ago. "I couldn't take my eyes off of you." His finger dipped lower, sliding to the valley between my breasts. "Imagine how surprised I was to be so drawn to you. And then for the council to..." Now he kissed me, all of the passion in his voice translating into the lip lock.

I kissed him back, hard, deep, passionately, and a new ache started low in my belly. My body was never going to get enough of this man. But he pulled back and leaned his forehead against mine. "I don't want you to be sorry."

I smiled. Crazy man. "I could never be sorry." It didn't make sense that I was unhappy, even a smidge at the council, but I didn't like having the power taken out of my hands, of being used as a pawn for those corrupt leaders. "But the council shouldn't be able to force us...I'm sorry that my ire at them is interrupting a moment like this."

"I agree. They shouldn't have." And then he grinned again. "But is it wrong that I'm glad they did?" He ducked his eyes. "Otherwise you might've taken years to come around."

I had to chuckle, then. He was right, in a way. I probably would've been content to be Jax's neighbor and girlfriend for a very long time. And I would've been missing out on this incredible feeling of being bonded to him. "I am, too." But despite the gratitude I felt for them as a group, the council's dynamic had never made sense to me. There was so much animosity and disturbing behavior, in-fighting, and arguments. My mish-mash of thoughts brought me around to, "I thought Soran hated Gretchen."

"Soran hates everyone. Or pretends to. His loyalties are clear only to Soran." Jax rolled his eyes. "He's a difficult man."

A fact I could believe based on his past behavior. Soran was a disagreeable, snotrag of a man, and every time I'd ever seen him, he'd been hard, but I'd suspected it was an act. Hearing Jax confirm it wasn't validation, but confirmation.

But hey, at least we thought alike.

CHAPTER FIVE

The night wasn't nearly long enough for all the things I wanted to talk about, all the things I wanted to do to him, with him. We made the most of it, only leaving the bedroom for a few minutes near dawn to drink some bagged blood. It was better than nothing, and we both felt depleted after a long night of lovemaking. And bonding.

I could feel his power inside of me now. And not because *he* was still inside me, physically. Or inside me *again*. But because this was one of the perks of our bond. It evened our power. Not totally yet, but it gave me strength and skills, and energy I wouldn't have had without the bond. More would come nightly as we continued sharing venom and blood.

My body hummed as we finished, as he kissed me softly and I tried not to roll him onto his back, not to exert the force it would take to be the one in control —he'd surrendered willingly so many times already— but I couldn't stop myself.

I pushed him onto his back then straddled his hips, love flowing through me from both my emotions and his as he smiled up at me.

"You feel it?" he asked.

Oh, baby. I felt so many things, but right now, my focus blurred, and I couldn't get around the surges and crescendos.

"I have all this energy." I held out my hand and showed it to him. There was no way I could keep it steady. I had the shakes.

He dragged my fingers to his lips and kissed each tip, then sat up. "Well, let's go for a run." He chuckled as I ground my hips absently in his lap.

I grinned. A run. Just what I needed, and we had a bit of time before dawn. Heck, I could run to Boston and back, probably, and I had that kind of energy right now.

But for now, we got dressed and took off. The city blurred past and before I could blink, we were across town, on Ben Franklin Parkway, running the steps, arms up at the top, dancing around like prizefighters. Then he grabbed me by the waist and spun me around. Laughing, I backed off, then danced around some more.

"Does it ever go away?" I asked, reveling in the moment.

He cocked an eyebrow.

"This feeling?" I prompted. "This power?"

He grinned, and it was better than I remembered lying on the beach to be. Brighter than I remembered the sun shining. I punched the air. Left, right, left, left, right. Rapid. Like I was Rocky.

Jax circled me, not moving as fast or as energized. He was used to this level of power. "You'll get stronger every night until you're as strong as I am," he said.

Oh, yeah! For a moment, I'd forgotten this wasn't all. This was just a taste.

But until what? I didn't necessarily want to test it, exactly but I would've bet I was close to Jax's levels, already. I'd never felt so capable. I smiled slyly and continued dancing around him. "Try me now."

He moved faster than I could *track* until he was in front of me and had my arms clasped in one hand over my head. Hooookay. His body was *close*. "Every time we exchange venom, you'll get stronger. And at the end of the moon cycle, you'll be my fully bonded mate." His tone turned serious, and he leaned his forehead against mine. "But until then, don't take chances. Don't try anything crazy."

"Hmm." I shot him a side-eye as much as I could with my hands over my head. "It sounds suspiciously as if you don't trust my strength." To demonstrate, I pulled free and moved him back a few steps by trying to strike the butt of my hand against his chest.

Before I made contact, though, he caught my wrist, spun me around, and pinned my arms against my chest. I couldn't have moved if I'd wanted to. "Soon. But not today." And then he let go. My body slumped, missing him instantly now that he was gone.

But it was game on. I sped through the town, always two steps behind, but *only* two steps, and that said something. Laughing, I burst forward, almost clasping his shoulder, but he saw me reach in time and put on his own extra surge of speed.

When we returned home, this time to mine and not his, I bounded onto the porch beside him, and he pulled me into a kiss. I hadn't been this giddy since I was a teenager talking to my first crush. It was hard to stand still in his embrace. Could we bounce and hug?

He grinned down at me and smoothed my hair. "It's time to get serious," he whispered. "You ready?"

I could've gone for a few more hours alone with his naked body, but I had a house full of vampires when I walked in—Luke and Ransom, Grim, Nash, and Paige.

Jax looked at them each in turn. Luke still had a bit of wide-eyed newness on his face, and I wanted to go to him, but he was already sitting so close to Ransom they might as well have been sharing skin. At least I had the peace of mind of trusting Ransom to be able to train Luke. He would do a great job.

"It's time to deal with the council." Jax sounded solemn like this wasn't a choice, but a duty. "And we need to get as many contacts as we can onboard. We need to find out who is with Soran and Gretchen and who isn't."

There were nods and smiles like this wasn't a new idea, just one that had finally gained some traction.

Paige nodded. "I've been mulling it over. What if we have a party? To present your new mate to the world and complete the mating ritual traditionally."

"Traditionally?" If this involved some kind of vampire orgy, I was out. A girl had to have boundaries.

Paige nodded. "There's an ending to the ritual. A blessing of sorts by the sires. Since Jax is your sire, only Dominic needs to give a blessing, which you already have, and being true-mates makes it a sure thing, but tradition is important to vampires."

Yeah. I was aware. They were annoyingly traditional.

"We could have the party at the gallery," Luke suggested. He was always up for a party at the place he loved the most.

But I hated the idea. "Not after last time." The gallery was the place where Soran and Gretchen had come for me and nearly killed Luke.

Jax looked at me. "I think it's a good idea to have the party, though. A power move."

He was right. It would show them we were unafraid, unaffected even. This was Luke's gallery, and we would party there at our leisure, unworried by their presence. This time, they would be invited, even. I sighed and nodded, but Luke and Ransom were already checking dates on Luke's phone calendar. They'd known I'd be talked into it, the finks. I expected my brother to be a little bit more subdued, but he was vibrant. Sparkling, even.

"The party needs to be in July. Before the end of the cycle." While Jax spoke, he continued to look at me.

Luke cocked his head and clapped his hands together. Nothing my bro liked more than a party.

Worry flared in my belly. "Luke." I shook my head as he glanced at me. "I'm sorry, brother, but if you go to the party, then the council will know that Ransom made you." I hated to say it because I liked his happiness, and how visual it was. "You have to stay hidden until we can make changes so that making new vampires isn't forbidden or controlled by the council."

Luke sighed and puffed out his lower lip into a pout. "Party pooper. Always have been, always will be." And no one I'd ever met did pouty better.

"I'll stay with Luke." Ransom smiled at my brother and the pout disappeared. All was right in Luke's world. For a second, at least. "But if they catch wind of him being alive, we need him to be able to at least moderately, with some sense of skill, be able to defend himself." He paused. "Then I won't have to worry so much." As if he'd only just heard himself, he shook his head. "We. We wouldn't have to worry so much." How cute.

Those were the most words I'd ever heard Ransom speak at one time. Probably more than he normally spoke in an entire day. He was the strong, silent type, heavy on the silence.

Of course, he was right, too, so it made the words all that much more important. Plus, they were an active demonstration of his feelings for my brother which made me happy for them both.

Before anyone else could speak or act, Jax pulled his phone from his pocket and dialed. Silence fell over the room until he spoke. "Dom, it's done. We're bonded, and we're having the traditional party." He paused to listen to whatever Dominic was saying. I could've focused and heard what Jax's maker was saying, but if he'd wanted to share with the room, he would've put it on speaker. "Yeah, yeah," Jax said. "It's going to be good for everyone. We'll see you on July Fourth." He took a couple more seconds more to listen, then nodded and smiled as if he was agreeing. "You bet." He hung up and looked at me. "Dom says hello."

Well, hey to Dom.

"Okay, so July Fourth?" I asked. "That gives us about a month to train Luke."

Luke bounded to his feet. "Let's do this! I'm ready."

Ransom grabbed his hand and pulled him back down. "It's about fifteen minutes until dawn. You're going to drop like a rock in a minute."

They said their goodbyes and headed to bed.

Jax and I followed soon after, getting ready for bed quietly and slipping between my sheets. "We'll continue our venom exchange," he murmured as my eyes got heavy. "And Luke can be training all that time."

I smiled sleepily. At least now we had a plan.

CHAPTER SIX

WEEK ONE

Luke's training was...a work in progress for sure.

WEEK TWO

More training for Luke.
It was not looking good. Progress was slow.

WEEK THREE

More training for Luke.
He was about as coordinated as a cooked noodle.
It still wasn't looking good.

WEEK FOUR

Luke was a *terrible* vampire.

CHAPTER SEVEN

There were about a thousand ways to get around the sun. The Michael Jackson umbrella wasn't nearly as effective as the Minnie Pearl hat, and the Moncler down coat probably provided the best coverage, but it was nearly July and hot. Even if the heat didn't bother me, the coat would've looked wrong.

So, I had my Rose-from-Titanic wide-brimmed hat with my hair tucked and hidden. It would burn like the rest of me if exposed. There was nothing I could do about how odd my gloves, long sleeves, jeans, and knee-high boots looked. I was dressed better for a chilly autumn day, but we had business in town that could only happen during human business hours.

Interestingly enough, nobody stared. No one pointed or laughed. All my high school fears, all the times I'd felt like everyone in the world was looking at me, were unrealized. I didn't know how much of that had to do with real-life self-absorption, or if it was Jax compelling them to not notice us, but we walked across the street from the parking lot, up the steps to the entrance of the courthouse. DA Robert Bevel had an entire floor of offices for himself and his ADAs.

The heat didn't bother me, other than the fear of turning into a crispy critter. Even once we were inside the building, the whole front was massive windows. Sunlight poured into the large room, no corner shadowy or safe for us.

Jax walked up to the reception desk and asked to speak to Bevel himself. The receptionist nearly laughed when he asked, but then a flat look crossed her face and she got on the phone. "Yes, sir," she whispered. "There's a man out here I think you need to speak with."

Bevel barked through the line, which I heard without trying. "I told you to hold any walk-ins today."

The pretty woman smiled nervously, then lowered her voice. "Sir, I wouldn't have interrupted your work unless it was urgent."

Jax leaned forward. I didn't have to hear his thoughts to know he was urging her to convince her boss to say yes.

"Sir," she pleaded.

A sigh came out of the earpiece. "Be right there."

About a minute later, Bevel stepped through a doorway. He was a tall guy with salt and pepper hair, thin in the middle, and he wore a scowl every time I'd seen him. This time was no different, even as he motioned us back to his office. He obviously recognized us and wasn't too happy about having to talk to us. Jax and crew had come to his office repeatedly while Luke was in the hospital, getting information on the case against Linda Hull, former kingpin of Philly.

I'd only been a few times, but it was often enough that Bevel knew me. We walked around the desk and through one of those gates that was meant to block the public, but a fifth-grade hurdler could've hopped over.

His office was lined on two walls with bookshelves crammed full of law books—not a Stephen King in the bunch—and a wall of windows behind his desk looked down on Philly. I pictured him spinning around to look outside, his high backed leather chair back facing the door as he pondered a problem with a case or something he had to deal with. This would have been the ideal place for quiet thought if the bustle and voices and creaks and squeal of things that needed oiled didn't come through the flimsy door.

Jax looked up at Bevel and smiled. "We're here to speak to you about the Linda Hull case." He spoke with authority and power, and it was *hot*. Of course, there was not much he did that I didn't think was hot. And it was even worse now that our bond was nearly complete. Our strength was almost matched, and I'd never been this close to another person. Not even my Lukey.

"What can I do for you, Mr. Parsons?" Bevel cocked a brow at Jax. "This time?"

"Word on the street"—and because he had the hearing of a bat— "is that Linda Hull confessed."

"Word on the street?" Bevel sat back in his chair and tented his fingers. Nobody in that room believed that word on the street was where Jax got his information, but also no one questioned more than that. "With Mr. Whitfield's testimony, the case should be a slam dunk."

I didn't want to tell him how to do his job—though, that was exactly why we were there—but no way could Luke testify. I couldn't risk my brother to the sunlight, not while he was this new of a vampire. Not to mention, this case was high profile. High profile meant press coverage at the courthouse steps. Voracious questioning. Jostling. And if just an inch of Luke's skin was exposed to the sun, one sizzle blew the whole game. No way we could take that kind of chance. And if it was on TV, we risked someone spotting Luke and recognizing him for what he now was.

Jax knew it, too. He stared hard at Mr. Bevel until Bevel's eyes glazed over. "Luke Whitfield won't be testifying," Jax said. "You don't need him."

Like he was in a trance, Bevel nodded. "I don't need him." His words came out casually, without inflection.

"You have plenty of evidence without Luke." Jax no doubt was repeating everything in Bevel's head, the way he'd taught me.

Bevel nodded. "So much evidence."

Jax's compelling game was on point. He'd wanted me to do this compelling for practice, but I'd talked him out of it. This was way too important.

Bevel smiled as Jax released his hold on the DA and we stood. I yawned because it was long past my sleeping time. I couldn't help it, but Jax smiled. "One more thing." He once again looked at Bevel. "Luke Whitfield will be of no value to your case even as a witness."

"I agree." Bevel nodded and stared at Jax as we walked to the door. I kept an eye on him to make sure he didn't snap out of this and try to stop us or have us arrested for interfering in an investigation or whatever lawyer mumbo jumbo he came up with.

Somehow, we escaped unscathed. Well, not somehow. Thanks to Jax's skills.

When we were downstairs in Jax's van and on the road, he looked at me as I yawned. The windows were tinted well beyond what was legal, but that was easy enough to deal with if we were pulled over.

Philly cops were easy for Jax to compel, but we were unbothered on the way back to his house. Nothing interrupted our drive but my yawns. He parked in the garage and the door slid shut behind us, closing us in darkness. With the sun off of the van, I relaxed and got even sleepier. We sat for a moment, and he brushed my hair off my forehead.

"Have I said how glad I am that you moved in across the street?" His voice had that butter-soft purring quality that made my stomach clench. Made my phantom heartbeat kick into gear, too.

"I think so." It was a flat miracle I could manage words at all. The combination of his hand on my face, his voice, and the close proximity in the car was heady.

"And have I said I love you today?" he asked.

He generally said it many times throughout every night. We weren't usually awake this time of day and it was a bonus.

"I always love hearing it." My voice was air-infused, more than its usual. Today I sounded downright breathy, porn-star breathy, and I couldn't help it. I was sleepy and overwhelmed by my mate.

"How about a nap?" He chuckled and got out of the car, coming around to open my door as I moved at a sloth's speed.

We had hours left to sleep. I followed him into the house, careful to avoid the windowed rooms as I headed to his bedroom.

Barely awake, I washed my face and brushed my teeth, then I was asleep in his arms almost as soon as we settled down.

CHAPTER EIGHT

When I walked into my house that night with Jax not far behind me, Ransom and Luke were already awake, sitting together on the couch. I was a little surprised to see them up this soon after dark. I checked the clock on my phone.

Oh. I'd spent more time in bed with Jax than I'd realized. In an attempt to make sure our bond was strong, and to be absolutely sure I'd end up as powerful as Jax, we'd taken to doing the venom exchange before bed and again as soon as we woke.

It'd been a sexually satisfying four weeks.

For as well as things had been going for me since I became a vampire—kick-ass job, new friends, a love life better than ever before in my life—things for Luke were shaky.

Luke had Ransom, but his gallery, the very first love of his life, was failing. He'd been trying to manage it with the help of a day manager, but between being gone for his training, his unavailability during the day to answer questions, and the fact that the new manager he'd hired didn't care nearly as much as Luke did, the place was failing.

"I don't know what to do, Hails." That wasn't something my very confident but currently shaken brother said often. Poor Luke. He was so upset about this. "You know how I love the gallery."

I did and nodded, but he wasn't even looking at me.

"He sold one of the local paintings that *wasn't for sale*. The artist was livid." He threw up his hands. "He's pulling the collection. And I have to refund the purchase price, *plus* the buyer wants a fee for his inconvenience."

I hated people like that, but I had an idea. "Maybe you could compel him to be a bit more reasonable." I wiggled my eyebrows. "There are some perks to our condition."

Luke sighed. "I tried." He shook his head and looked down at his blue suede shoes that matched his blue suede pants and the blue suede jacket he was wearing with a shirt that had more ruffles than Frito-Lay. "He clubbed me with his cane, called me gay Elvis, then shoved me out the door."

A pompadour and the shoes would've been enough to earn the Elvis jab, but Luke had been setting off gay-dar since he turned ten and first wore eyeshadow.

"How much does he want?" I asked. Not like I was going to let Luke pay anyone much more than they paid for the painting, but I was curious.

"He paid ten and wants an extra ten for his trouble." He threw his hands up. "Of course."

"Ten grand?" I asked, aghast.

Luke nodded.

"I offered to talk to him." Ransom scowled, and it had to be killing him to let Luke handle this on his own, especially with how horribly Luke was taking all this.

Luke shot him a look. That was a warning if I'd ever seen one. "It isn't just this. I can get the painting back, and of course, I'm not giving the guy ten grand. But what's to keep it from happening again?"

Uh-oh. The whine meant he was in a mood even I couldn't bring him back from.

He hung his head. "I'm going to sell."

"Oh, Luke," I whispered.

That gallery had been his dream. He'd worked and bled and sweated for it. Anyone who knew Luke knew he hated to sweat, but for the gallery, he'd suffered through it.

He lifted his eyes. "Don't give me that disappointed-in-Luke sigh, Hails. I just don't think I can take it." He sniffed and dabbed at his eyes with a tissue that previously looked like a part of his shirt.

"Oh, honey." I moved to sit beside him and put my arm around him, hugging him close. "I'm not disappointed *in* Luke. I'm disappointed *for* Luke, sweetheart." I laid my head on his shoulder. "In third person."

He smiled, almost. "Maybe I can find a buyer who loves it as much as I do."

I rubbed his back in slow circles. "If you're sure this is what you want, then I hope so." Luke had been a shining star in our family since I could remember. I hated seeing him so unhappy.

"We should find another place for the party." Jax looked solemn but realistic. "If you're selling, we probably shouldn't count on hosting it there." He stood and went into the kitchen to make his call.

Luke sighed and dialed his phone. We'd dug it out after the first night home. "No point in putting it off," he muttered.

When the person on the other end answered, he went full Luke, his voice a cross of professional and sexy. "Nadia, darling, it's the man of the hour and he needs a favor." He listened for a minute then laughed like he didn't have a care in the world. "No. I don't want to date your cousin Smith." He laughed. "I'm *involved*." He drew the word out and winked at Random, who stared stoically back at him.

There was a very definite squeal from the earpiece, and he held the phone away. "Of course, he's a darling." He placed a hand on Ransom's arm. "You're going to love him. Now, about my favor." He detailed the terms of his sale and then hung up. "Fine. It's done." And gone was the man of the hour and back was the man of the mope.

"I hope you didn't do that lightly," I whispered, throwing my hands around him again.

"No," he moaned. "It's been coming since I was hurt. Being away for so long and having the gallery closed was a massive financial hit." He shrugged. "The good news is that I have the building paid off and the inventory is on commission. The sale will be pure profit." Tears pooled in his eyes, and he slumped from my arms into Ransom's. I got up and paced, agitated at my brother's dream going down the toilet.

Not that I could blame him. This wasn't what he'd signed up for. Giving up everything he'd ever wanted, settling for never again seeing the sun or his summer tan. He'd so loved a golden glow.

Poor Luke. But then, he settled onto the sofa and tipped his head back to stare at the ceiling. It needed a coat of paint, but before he could comment, or perhaps offer to do the work, his cell rang.

He answered without ever looking away from my ceiling, then sat forward. "Already? ...An online offer? But I didn't set an asking price." He paused and listened. "Very generous." He mouthed, "Oh my God," at me then began nodding as if the caller could see. "You're an angel. Just bring the contract to me, tomorrow night. I'll be tied up all day. Could we meet at nine?" He laughed, almost giddy. "Nothing good in the world happens before nine p.m., darling."

When he hung up, he squealed at me and Ransom, and I widened my eyes. "Well?"

"She put out a feeler, and immediately got an offer that is about five times what I would've set as asking price." He shimmied his shoulders. "I'm in the money. Even after I repay my savings from the time being closed." He stood and turned a full circle, jumping up and down. When he stopped, he smoothed the jacket, adjusted the ruffled sleeves, and cleared his throat. "It's very good news. And she said it was a short sale, so money soon." He plopped down in front of Random. "With this kind of money, we can start up anything we want to. The sky's the limit!"

But part of me was still sad. This had been his life-long dream.

Fortunately for him, so was being stinking rich and from the sound, he was going to be doing okay after the sale.

At just the moment Luke stopped celebrating, Jax walked in. He raised his eyebrows but didn't ask. Instead, he sat on the chair across from me. "I called everyone. We have to rework the party, I assume."

Luke nodded, still grinning, but not gushing. It was probably killing him. Luke was a natural-born gusher.

When Paige, Grim, and Nash arrived with Cleo and Kendra, we moved to the kitchen table like we were some sort of nocturnal board of directors party-planning committee.

They'd been on a skip. We'd been balancing everything going on with Luke with our skip traces in an attempt to keep the money flowing.

Luke outlined the issue about having the party at the gallery. Since it was now sold, he couldn't risk a full-out vampire shindig since it wasn't his place. When a large group of vamps came together in one place, there was sometimes chaos. No one knew that better than us.

"What about the backyard?" Paige nodded toward my front door, but she meant Jax's backyard, across the street. It was spacious and fairly level, cared for by a landscaping company who mowed and trimmed and planted and pulled weeds from around the flowers and bushes.

It would be easy to move most of the obstacle course and training grounds. They'd been put to good, if pointless, use with training Luke.

My darling brother was a breathtakingly beautiful vampire, with the color of his skin somehow glowing rather than pasty, but he hadn't picked up any of the physical stuff *at all*. Like...nothing. He still punched like a Victorian lady.

We all looked at Jax. It was his party, his yard, and we needed his say. Of course, it was my party, too, but his place, so I remained silent while he did the thinking.

"The party is in four..." He checked his watch. "No, three days. The yard is, well, it needs work."

Paige shook her head. "It isn't that bad. And you have the night-blooming jasmine, the gardenia augustus..." Paige listed a few more flowers that Jax had recently requested the gardeners plant because he wanted me to have flowers to look at. I'd thought it was corny at the time, but every once in a while, when I looked out and saw the blooms, or if we were outside sparring, I fell a little more in love.

"We can have a good old American Fourth of July barbecue. Less formal. More relaxed." Paige smiled. "I love a good barbecue."

"Me, too," Kendra said, walking in the front door like she owned the place. I didn't mind. She was my bestie after all. "I don't suppose I could invite a few witch friends?"

Jax shrugged. "The guest list will be mostly vampires, so there wouldn't be a big call for traditional grilled foods, but it'll help set the mood if we do have some things grilling."

Kendra nodded eagerly. "I'd be happy to help cook, too."

Jax nodded toward Cleo. "Of course, you're invited, Ms. Cleo, but I'll have to say no to Jordan. He only knows about the witches. Not the vampires."

Nash looked at Jax. "So long as I don't have to man the grill. You know the smell of human food makes me ill."

Jax nodded. "You can be in charge of drinks." He winked at Kendra, then nodded to Grim. "Grim can cook." Once upon a time, he'd been a chef. He still loved to cook. Jax glanced at me. "Can you send out e-vites and let the humans know about the change in plans? Paige has the guest list. I'll take care of the vampires."

I was confused. "There are going to be humans?"

Jax nodded. "Some from the club." Jax's club, Catch & Release, was where vamps could go for a quick bite, err, sip, or a pint of bagged blood. Those who opted for the bite could choose from any number of volunteer humans. But it was strange to discuss them like this. For me, anyway. For Jax, it was probably normal. That was one of the things I was going to have to get used to. Maybe one day.

Kendra smiled. "I have a few fairy friends who will happily come and provide some lighting." Nothing in the world made a night prettier than honest-to-goodness fairy lights made by honest-to-goodness fairies. Coolest thing ever.

Jax smiled at her. "Perfect. Now we have a plan." He stood. "We'd better get to work." He glanced at me. "Hails, don't forget to put the theme on the e-vite."

A theme? But it was his shindig, a vampire thing that I was so new at, so I nodded. "All right. What is it?"

He spread his hands like it was the most obvious thing in the world. "Fourth of July, of course. Americana."

And so the preparations began.

CHAPTER NINE

July 4

Nothing like a party to bring a bunch of bloodthirsty vampires together. I smiled at Jax as he arranged blood. He'd asked that it be poured into what would appear to anyone else as beer. He was going all-in with this shindig, and I was impressed with his attention to detail. The blood-beer had labels that could have easily been on any bottle of beer in any grocery store, cleverly titled Clotmans.

A red, white, and blue banner hung from one corner of the yard to the opposite against the fence line, and the fairies had arrived and gave the place an ethereal glow. This wasn't like any barbeque I'd ever been to.

Maybe in Texas.

Our hands brushed as Jax put more Clotmans into the warming bucket—98.6 was the optimal temp. We smiled at one another, which was nothing new. It seemed like all we did lately was look googly-eyed. It was starting to drive our friends a little crazy, not that we cared. Being around Jax now that our bond was pretty much complete was my happy place.

"You have Luke on speed dial?" Jax asked.

Telling my brother he couldn't come to the party hadn't been easy. Watching him take it so well because he was getting used to giving things up since he was now a vampire was even harder. It made me sad. So, I'd promised to sneak pictures when I could and to call him as soon as everyone left and fill him in.

"Of course." He'd been number one in my phone, then Kendra, then Jax. Silly sentiment had me move Jax to the top a few days ago.

Jax grinned one of those smiles that said he'd been up to something sneaky. "I had Grim and Nash put cameras in the yard so Luke can watch the party live-action streaming."

The love I had for this guy grew by the minute. If it wasn't his thoughtfulness, his protectiveness, or the way he looked in basketball shorts, it was every single other thing about him. "He'll love that," I murmured, fully aware my eyes were all goo-goo-ey again.

"Good." Jax walked back to a table arranged with party favors: flags, noisemakers with red, white, and blue streamers, and some of those snap pop things kids liked—little bits of gunpowder that exploded on impact with the ground when thrown. They were pretty good fun. I'd wasted a whole box of them last night when Jax brought them home.

We had a small setup for the big fireworks for later in the night. When I said big, I mean the ones that weren't legal to have in a residential neighborhood, but who was going to tell a group of vamps that they weren't allowed to have them.

Well, they could try. It didn't mean they'd be successful.

The guests were due to arrive soon, so all we had to do at this point was wait. Nerves jangling, I spent my time waiting with Jax in one corner of the kitchen. At the table, Paige, Nash, and Grim had their headsets on and waited for the guests to start arriving. The looks on their faces ranged from stoic to nervous. Of course, it was Grim and Nash looking stoic. Paige would have this stuff in hand, no doubt, but she looked apprehensive about it.

Jax squeezed my hand as the first guests started to arrive. The human volunteers were roaming the yard, enjoying frozen beverages, some alcoholic, some not, and barbecued meats and vegetables. Some of them I recognized from Catch and Release.

We walked out of the gate from the backyard to the front and stood beside the carpet. It was a red carpet, of sorts. It was made of red and white checked gingham, rather than a deep red. It'd been Luke's idea, and I had to admit it was incredibly cute.

Oh, my heavens. My attention landed on a woman stepping out of a limo parked at the curb. We advanced to her as she adjusted the ball gown she wore so it wouldn't get stuck in the limo door. When she was satisfied with the gown, she met us halfway with her head high and her hand out to Jax, knuckles up. Of all the... she expected him to kiss her hand. What was this, Victorian England?

I fought against the urge to punch her. Jax was my mate. *Mine!*

He obliged and she gushed, simpering until he righted himself. He turned toward me and paused. His nostrils flared out a little as if he was scenting my jealousy, then a slow smirk formed. "Hailey, allow me to introduce Ms. Meredith Bird. Meredith is the leader of the northeast United States territories."

This woman wore a ball gown complete with crinoline and hoops underneath. That wasn't the most eye-widening part. The whole thing looked to be made from an American flag. Hopefully not *literally* a flag, but there was a star-spangled top, the very full skirt was red and white striped. Holy goodness. It must've been a big flag. Not because the woman herself was big, but because the skirt was at least three feet wide, maybe more. The more I looked at the dress, the more sure I was that the material had once been an actual flag. Talk about faux-pas.

"Hello," I murmured, trying not to look shocked by her dress. "It's lovely to meet you."

Meredith inclined her head ever so slightly, and I was seriously scared for the stay-ability of her coal-black hair, piled on her head in an early colonial hairdo of pin curls and tendrils. At least her smoky eye was on point.

Jax directed her to the beverage table, and I looked at the closest camera—the one in the front corner of the yard—and gave it an *Oh My Gawd* because that was a *dress*.

And since the night had only just begun, I couldn't *wait* to see what else the guests were serving up as their Americana wardrobe.

Before I had much time to recover, the limo moved out of the way, and a stretched...truck? Was that a truck? It looked like someone took a king-cab Ford truck and stretched it out into a limo. And I couldn't be sure, but the bed seemed like it could double as a hot tub.

Whatever the vehicle was called, it pulled up in the limo's place. Jax leaned in to whisper, "You're going to love this guy."

A large man with a cape that was far more quilt than cape exited the truck-thing and strode toward us. His cape looked as if it had been stitched in the mountains, by some granny-woman somewhere near Dollywood. A broad grin spread across the man's face as he stopped in front of Jax and held out his hand. "Jaxon, how interesting to see you again."

Oh, what an accent this guy had. He sounded as if a plate of cornbread was going to fall out of his mouth the next time he opened it.

Definitely interesting. And a hand-stitched quilt certainly fit the theme of America. I smiled next to Jax who gazed down at me. "Hailey, this is Rogan Henry, the leader of Tennessee and North Carolina." Oh, now the quilt made sense. Rogan was a tall, handsome black man in a finely tailored suit with the aforementioned cape. Upon my further inspection, the cape had music notes quilted into the pattern. Oh, fitting. Nashville. Cute.

I shook his outstretched hand. It was as soft as butter-like he spent more time than me lotioning. That was entirely possible considering I was always forgetting lotion. I was no better about it now that I was a vampire. "It's a pleasure to meet you," I said brightly.

He still had a wide smile on his face as he kissed my hand. "The pleasure, I assure you, is all mine,"

Rogan said in a rich, deep voice. There was something suggestive in his tone, so I looped my other hand around Jax's arm. Rogan was an intensely attractive man, but there was no swaying me from Jax.

When Rogan moved on and further into the yard to talk to the American flag lady, I turned to Jax. "He's something."

Jax smiled with laughter barely concealed behind his lips. "They all are. You're going to be fine."

I wasn't so sure. This was the first time I'd ever met any of them, and I was getting them all at once. It was a little overwhelming.

Our next guest arrived before I could get too worried. At least her limo was just normal if luxurious-looking. She glided across the gingham carpet toward us. "Jannah Swanson," Jax said. "So lovely to see you again." He leaned in and pressed a kiss against her cheek.

Jannah was tall and beyond gorgeous, makeup that looked like she'd spent hours having it professionally applied so that it would look effortless, and her slinky dress had lights, actual blinking lights.

"Hailey, this is Jannah and she is the leader of Las Vegas." Of course. The lights were neon-ish. She was representing her area of Vegas.

"The dress is clever," I said with a bright smile. "Given your territory."

Without acknowledging my compliment, Jannah shook my hand and gave me an up and down that found me sorely lacking if her grimace and barely concealed eye roll meant anything at all.

I had to fight not to look down at my shorts to make sure I hadn't somehow spontaneously changed into a potato sack or something. Geez. I straightened my spine. No way I was showing this woman she'd unnerved me. "Jax has told me so much about you." It was a small lie, but one I figured I could get away with.

Jax poked me in the back and Jannah smiled, although it was more sneer than a smile. "Did he, now? Did he tell you he spent some time with me in Las Vegas a couple of years ago?"

Uh-oh. I just stepped in that one. Served me right for trying to front to her. "Well, we're certainly glad you're here." With those words, I slipped my arm around Jax's waist. Just in case *spent time with me in Las Vegas* meant what she was implying it meant. She needed to understand that we took this bond very seriously.

And when she walked away to sink her vamp claws into poor Rogan Henry, and we had half a moment, Jax turned to me with his eyebrows raised and hands up. "Just a friend."

I nodded. "Uh-huh." Not that I doubted him. He was mine now and wouldn't lie. But giving Jax a hard time was fun, and I so rarely got the chance.

"Hailey..." He tangled his hand in my hair and tugged me forward until our lips met. "I have you, and you are all I will ever need."

I'd heard rumors about the mating bond being mostly about the mating and less about being together as two people who wanted to be together. Now wasn't the time to discuss it, though. Although, unless I could figure out how to push past the rumor on my own, the chat would have to happen at some point. I needed to know this feeling would last. I never wanted to lose it.

I wasn't teasing him because I was jealous. Much.

Okay, a little.

I smiled and yanked him back similarly to how he'd just done me. "I'm teasing," I muttered. "But I'm glad it's clear you're mine."

More guests arrived, cutting off his reply, though the growl deep in his throat didn't go unnoticed. The most interesting characters had arrived first, and I soon lost track of who was who, but I'd never seen so much denim and flannel in July, despite living in America my entire life.

Although I wasn't one to talk. I'd dressed in cut-off shorts and a flannel crop top tied just under my, er, at the top of my stomach. Heck, I'd even put in pigtail braids because it fit the outfit, along with boots Jax had gifted me that morning.

I met the leader of the Dakotas, dressed like a farmer, with overalls and even a long piece of wheat in his mouth. And then the chief of Los Angeles, which was such a big city that it got its own leader. He showed up with a t-shirt that had an actual movie playing on the front.

Gaping, I leaned in closer. "Is that Sweet Home Alabama?" I asked, incredulous and more than a little impressed.

He chuckled. "It is." Reese Witherspoon was southern-girling it across this guy's chest. Holy cannoli. Tech and fashion had found their meeting place.

"I love it," I declared before LA's honcho walked into the backyard. His name had totally left my mind, but he winked as he went past. More friendly than flirtatious.

And then it was time for the council to arrive, fashionably late, of course. And unfashionably dressed, according to the party theme anyway. There was nothing Americana about basic black. Tuxedos. Little black dresses. Sunglasses flipped down even in the dead of night.

And then Dominic stepped out of the limo. Sweet sweating summertime, he'd taken the theme to heart. Dominic was an attractive man on any given day. But in a full cowboy get up? Hoo-ha.

A shirt with pearl snaps on the pockets.

Spurs.

A ten-gallon hat.

And the *boots*. The boots deserved an entire monolog description I didn't have time for because my giggles were too hard to suppress. It was best to ignore the thoughts on his attire. He simultaneously looked devastatingly gorgeous and completely ridiculous. Like a hero on the cover of a romance novel, but out in the real world, it was way too much.

He kissed my cheek as I fought to hold in the laughter. "You're adorable, Hailey. Like you belong in Hazard County or at the Clampetts mansion in Beverly Hills."

I knew the references and laughed because no way in hell would I ever have guessed Dominic ever watched either show. How cute imagining him sacked out on the couch, watching the Beverly Hillbillies.

Poor Jax couldn't hold it in. Finally giving in, he busted out a laugh that echoed through the night and had his other guests turning to him. I took a glance over my shoulder at the camera and shrugged at my brother, who I just *knew* was sitting in his hotel room, where they were staying *many* miles away from here, live streaming the whole thing. He and

Ransom were likely falling all over each other laughing.

Although now that I thought about it, had I ever seen Ransom laugh? Surely at least once or twice.

Dominic stood in front of Jax, his lips pursed. "I feel a bit overdressed," he mumbled.

Jax got his laughter under control but couldn't stop his lips from twitching. "Not at all. You understood the assignment." He motioned to the yard. "Unlike the other council members." The sea of black mingled with the ocean of color and the party was in full swing.

Jax stared at Dominic as they spoke, but I stared at Jax. What that man did for a pair of Wranglers was magazine ad worthy, and while his boots weren't quite of the cowboy variety, they went with the outfit. His red and black flannel over an AC/DC t-shirt was a beautiful distraction from having to advertise our private business to the council.

He stepped onto the back patio. It lifted him enough so he could see the entire crowd. "Hailey and I want to thank everyone for coming to help us celebrate the mating bond ritual." He looked at me and winked and smiled. He continued, but I couldn't hear him anymore.

I was immersed in the love I felt for him, both mine and his coming through the bond. Even though we'd been pushed to do this quickly, it was the best thing I'd ever done.

"So in short..."

"Too late!" someone shouted from the back of the yard. Oh, whoops. While I'd been enthralled, he'd been droning on, maybe a bit more than was necessary.

Jax grinned. "Yeah, sorry. Anyway, thanks for coming, and have a good time." I loved his happiness as much as I loved the power he wore these days, the decisions he made, the way he loved me back.

This was the best decision I'd ever made. I was sure of it.

CHAPTER TEN

The entire time we moved around the yard, mingling and talking to the vampire guests, Jax kept his hand at the small of my back. If he moved his hand, it was to entwine his fingers with mine, and once or twice he dragged me to a dark corner for a quick kiss. We were in that sweet spot where everything felt new and perfect, and we weren't wasting it.

The barbecue was a front for making sure that we would have allies and backup when we took on the council, of course. Also, it was a way to prove to the council that we'd bonded. After this, they couldn't question anything.

We spoke first with Jannah. I thought maybe Jax should talk to her alone, that I would only make matters complicated or awkward, but he wouldn't let me out of it. "Come on," he murmured. "Our guests are waiting for us."

"Jax, this is a lovely party. It's refreshing to attend something..." She waved her hand. "Rustic. Not so stuffy." Backhanded compliment? Yeah. Oh, well.

Jannah had already sampled several of the humans and currently had her arm around a tall, dark drink of...ahem...*water* from the club. If I'd been single, I might've partaken myself. The guy was pretty hot. My gaze drifted over to Jax. Every other man paled in comparison. And that was saying something considering how fair-skinned Jax was.

"Hailey and I were wondering if you have a minute to speak privately." He nodded once, and Mr. Tall Dark walked away so it was just the three of us.

"Now that you've run my dinner away, what can I possibly do for you?" Her tone was less than friendly, as was the narrow-eyed glare she aimed at me. Geez, she was downright icy.

"We need to talk about the council and we're looking for support," Jax spoke softly because vampires had big ears and weren't afraid of using them. Everyone else was in a big group conversation near the house or inside. I didn't think they'd hear us.

"Oh, Jaxon." She shook her head, and it was as much an insult as if she'd come out and called him stupid. "The council protects us. They make sure we're safe from those who would have us extinguished before we could even speak and promise not to hurt anyone." Her sigh came out fast and loud like she was trying to attract attention. Not to mention the flashing lights on her dress were extremely eye-catching in the dim fairy lights all over the shadowy yard. "Let's not start this conversation, yes?"

I laid a hand on Jax's arm when he tensed. "Of course. Thank you for coming. Have a good time tonight." I led Jax away because there was no talking to Jannah. Her mind was made up. She didn't even hesitate before shutting Jax down. Jannah Swanson was one hundred percent pro-council.

As we caught people alone for quiet moments, it became increasingly obvious that they all thought the same as Jannah. Either they rebuffed Jax completely or they brushed him off with a subject change. Each rejection was a stab to the gut. A defeat.

Poor Jax. He tried everything. To Rogan, who Jax had told me was a romantic at heart, he made a point to say, "I wasn't at all happy that our mating bond had a timeline. An expiration date. It took the choice out of our hands and became more like force." While Rogan had seemed sympathetic, he'd changed the subject quickly.

We headed over to the leader of the Dakotas, Stuart, and Jax said, "It would've been ideal to have had the time to plan for the bonding ritual, to be able to make time to do it better." He added a look at me. I wasn't sure if it was meant to be an apology or if it was part of his convincing the others act. But it was solemn and adorable. One I would try to remember to thank him for later.

"Well," Stuart said. "Unfortunately, those have been the rules for many years."

And thus was the theme of the night. We got answers like, "Yeah, maybe, but no one wants to take on the council, me included." That one from Paul, the Los Angeles commander with another state-themed movie playing on his shirt. I squinted as he cleared his throat and looked around, obviously uncomfortable.

"Is that Blue Hawaii?" I asked, squinting at Elvis gyrating on the screen.

Paul chuckled. "Of course. Gangs of New York is next. The newer one, with Leo."

Jax opened his mouth and leaned toward Paul, but, as if he knew Jax was going to talk about the council, stiffened and moved back a hair. His body language said extreme discomfort.

"Come," I said, sparing Paul and Jax both. We needed allies, but not by force. That route would only give us potential betrayers.

And before we could corner anyone else, it was time for the ritual part of the mating bond. Dominic, in his ten-gallon hat, stepped forward. "Friends," he called quietly. That was all it took for him to get everyone's attention. Everyone moved forward to stand on the back patio where Jax had given his speech. Moving to the front, Jax and I faced one another with Dominic behind us in the middle. It was not unlike a wedding, if not as formal. I had a feeling half of those in attendance would've rather it had been far more ceremonious than this.

The council watched, along with the other vampires, as Dominic joined my hands with Jax's and wrapped them in a thick, braided, silky cord. As he leaned forward, his hat fell off and bounced in front of us, then rolled down the steps and finally stopped at Rogan Henry's boot tip.

Laughter bubbled up my throat. I barely choked it back as I looked at Jax.

Dominic cleared his throat and must have moved his foot, too, because his spurs rattled like little jingling bells. I chewed my lip, and Jax's mouth twitched. Dominic in this getup, performing such a solemn ritual was amusing in a way I didn't understand but didn't fight either.

Dominic cleared his throat, again, glaring at me hard enough that I wiped my smile. Jax, on the other hand, didn't. He whispered, "Best day of my life, and not because of Dominic's ridiculous outfit." His words made my phantom pulse throb. And then my smile had nothing to do with Dominic or the fabric he was wrapping around our wrists.

"This cord is braided of three strong pieces of silk. One for power, one for strength, and one for love."

He looked from me to Jax and back again. "Good luck, you."

My laughter bubbled up again. "Thank you."

He took a chalice from Paige and held it out to Jax. We had to share blood. The process felt intimate, personal, and not something I wanted to do in front of the vampire world gathered in Jax's backyard, but since it was part of the ritual, my only choice had been to choose a chalice instead of drinking straight from the tap, or in this case a vein.

We'd ordered one off of Amazon. The chalice, not a vein.

Hey, it was a backyard bonding cup, not the Holy Grail.

After we each drank from the golden cup, Jax leaned in and kissed me. Not anything over the top or supremely decadent, but just perfect enough. A momentary touching of our lips that meant so much more than that. It was our commitment to one another. It was proof to the vampires and the council, but at this moment, on this night, they didn't matter in the least. All that mattered was Jax and me, and the fact that we were going to compete the bond.

Then, a long look in one another's eyes, and then we were back to moving around the party, although now with fewer politics and more light touches. Suddenly, I couldn't keep my hands off of him and damn sure couldn't wait for everyone to go home.

The party dragged on a few more hours, then it was *finally* time for everyone to go. I thanked the creatures of the night, every one, as they left, but I was extremely glad to see the taillights that indicated their departures.

And finally, after *another* couple of hours, when the yard was cleaned and put back together, I sat on the sofa beside Jax and put my head on his shoulder. "A good night?"

He slung his arm around me and kissed the top of my head. "A very good night."

"Even though we didn't end up with any allies to help us with the council?" It would've been nice to know someone was on our side. It was why he'd decided to host this party, mainly. We could've just invited the council over to witness the bond. Or gone to them.

"Some could come back." He sighed. "It was a lot to discuss while so much evil was lurking." He was, of course, referring to the council and their supersonic hearing.

I nodded, although I couldn't stop the sadness in my stomach that we seemed to be alone in this fight. All by ourselves.

Heck, while one or two vampires on our side would've been a start, it wouldn't have been enough. If we were going to take on the council, we needed more vampires to take up the cause. And that was going to take work.

Joy.

CHAPTER ELEVEN

Grim and Nash had spent their time at the party—the time they weren't busy making sure everything went off without a hitch—putting out feelers, trying to get more support for our cause. Unfortunately, they'd come up as short as Jax and me.

Yay.

"No one wants to take on the council." Grim shook his head in disgust. "They're all freaking scared."

Nash stood beside him in the doorway between the kitchen and living room with his arms crossed. "Most agree that the council is overbearing, wrong even, and they all give off a rebel vibe like they want to join in an uprising or something." He clarified quickly, "But not enough to do anything about it." He exchanged a glance with Grim. "I think though, if you start the fire, they'll fan the flames."

Right around that moment, the front door opened, and Luke and Ransom walked in. Luke looked a bit more like his usual self, though without the color in his cheeks. He was dressed like a cowboy, more like Dominic's cowboy than Jax's, except Luke was wearing actual cowskin. As in, it looked like hide, rather than a sleek leather.

He plopped onto the sofa behind me. "I missed a gala soiree." He was one grimace from a growl.

I laid my hand on his. "It wasn't that great." It was torturous after the ritual. I'd just wanted to run off with Jax and smooch.

Maybe more.

He clutched his hands over his heart. "Three braided cords? A ritual to make you two a couple?" He shook his head. "And I couldn't be here to share it with you."

New Luke was a bit more bitter than human Luke. My heart squeezed that he hadn't been there. He was right about that. He should've been. I patted his leg. "It was..." *Who am I kidding?* "It was amazing. A moment."

His hair brushed my chin as he rested his head on my shoulder for a moment before sitting up again. "I know. I saw you gushing at him." He made a face and tried to smile but looked constipated instead. "Life *is* surprising." The resentment in his tone caused an ache in my stomach.

Jax looked around me to give Luke a sympathetic expression. "It's going to get better, Luke. You'll see."

Luke scoffed and sat back.

Ransom hadn't moved far into the room, and I wondered if Luke's dour mood had affected them, but I didn't ask. If Luke wanted me to know, he would tell me.

"As you were saying about the council?" Ransom asked.

"Nobody will speak out against the council." Jax shrugged. "We'll think of something else."

Ransom shook his head. "Of course, they wouldn't speak against the council with the council within earshot."

His tone was so sarcastic I laughed before I could stop myself. He shot Jax a glaring eye roll, then shook his head. "They won't risk the danger. However, if you go at them each one by one, you might get a straight and honest answer."

Jax looked away then back at Ransom. "Couldn't you have mentioned that before I wasted a night playing host to the casts of *Twilight* and *True Blood* ?" Despite his aggravated tone, he shook his head and laughed. "But it is a good idea."

I wasn't sure which idea he meant, but I yawned. Last week, I'd managed to stay up an entire day, and I'd been happy to do it, proud when I made it from sunset to sunset, *and* another sunrise before sleep came for me, but now it'd been a very long night. I was tired, and I wanted to go to bed.

With Jax. It was, in a way, our honeymoon, after all.

Luke had already crashed while we talked. Ransom smiled down at him, and brushed a lock of hair off his forehead, then lifted him as if Luke weighed nothing. To Ransom, he probably was pretty much weightless. I smiled at Ransom as he passed. Luke would find happiness again. I hoped so, anyway.

And my brother and I would talk about it soon because we had to. But right now, I had another someone I wanted to speak to, be with, and love.

When everyone went their separate ways and we were alone, Jax smiled at me, then leaned back against the sofa as if he was as tired as I was. He might've been, though he rarely showed it. "Linda's trial is over. They found her guilty yesterday."

It made sense he'd waited to tell me until after the party. I would've been distracted all night.

Anger bubbled in my stomach for the woman who'd shot and nearly killed my brother. She deserved prison for as many years as she had left on the Earth. Or even better, she deserved to be dinner.

Hey, don't be shocked. I'm a vampire now. Eating people is a part of it, however humane we try to keep it.

But Jax wasn't finished. "They couldn't try her for Luke's shooting because he couldn't testify."

That had been our doing. Not much I could've done about that, anyway.

Jax took my hand, and we walked to his room. "Ransom carried Luke." I pretended to be miffed that he wasn't carrying me, but just being near Jax was enough for me at this point.

He nodded, a ghost of a smile on his lips. "If I carried you, I couldn't back you against the wall and kiss you until you can't breathe."

I smiled because there was nothing I liked more than being pressed between him and... well, anything. The wall, a piece of furniture, the shower door, whatever. "I don't need to breathe."

He shook his head and turned me quickly so that my back pressed against the wall nearest his bedroom door. A week ago, it would've been faster than I could've tracked. Now, it felt just as normal as if we'd both been human moving at human speed.

"No, you don't have to, but I love that you still do it. That the human parts of you are still so," He moaned as he leaned in and kissed me softly, then pulled back and tapped the spot over my heart. "Right here."

I sighed in perfect peace and contentment. Jaxon Parsons wasn't just any guy who'd found his way into my Levi's. He was *the* guy. His second kiss was powerful and potent and had the strength of a thousand kisses behind it.

He walked us into the bedroom, and I let my hands roam the planes of muscles under his shirt. I took a moment to delight in the way I could still sense the warmth that was once there.

This time he did scoop me into his arms and carried me to the bed, then set me on my feet to give me a look. The look was chock full of emotions. They could've been worship; could've been love. Heck, they could've meant any number of things. But right now, my focus narrowed to Jax. To his tapered waist, his broad chest, the way he moved his body.

The kiss he laid on me was electric and vibrant, and damn sure made me yearn. He had that power, easily. We'd been doing this every night for almost a month and still, I wanted him like it was brand new, like every time was the first time. Every kiss had the magic of a first kiss. Every...well, you get the picture, but in case you haven't yet: His arms were my safety, his body my playground, his pleasure dynamic because it was shared.

I kissed him as I took him inside me, and then I lost myself in every feeling, every sensation. The glorious friction of his body against my body. He was beauty, and power and intelligence and love all put together in a man so perfect—at least, I hadn't discovered a real flaw yet—it took my breath away.

He took my breath away.

When we each cried out and clung to one another, I did breathe, because it really felt like I needed to.

By the time we collapsed beside one another in the bed, the dawn light peeked around the edges of the curtains on the far side of the room, but sleep claimed me then, and I didn't care.

CHAPTER TWELVE

It was a joy to be back at work with Cleo and Kendra. Paige came along when we needed muscle, but the past few weeks had been low-dollar easy skips. Nothing to shatter the earth.

I took as much time off as possible and spent my evenings with Jax, practicing, learning how to use my new powers. Today was no different. My powers, since the bonding ritual, had cemented themselves inside of me. But there were so many, they affected me easily. Some things I didn't know how to deal with, and I was too overwhelmed to ask for his help. I wanted to be a put-together woman, a queen on top of my issues, and in control of the scope of what I could do.

Most of the time, I left my hearing off, sort of muted, but my sense of smell was more than I could deal with. I'd thought being a vampire meant I would forgo most of the human afflictions like nausea, but certain smells—gasoline, burned popcorn, and fish, to name a very few—turned my stomach every time. Oh, and rotten trash, ugh. So gross. Being in the city was the worst for a newly-powerful vampire.

It was not all bad. Not by a long shot. The best part, the absolute most incredible bit was the strength. And today, to my delight, Jax had brought us all to Norman's Junk in the Trunk. As in the trunks of the smashed junk cars that were stacked two stories high in piles.

Grim and Nash were like kids in the candy store. "I'm going to throw one farther than you are," Nash said quietly.

With a snort, Grim shoved at Nash. "Whatever, man. I always outdo you here."

Their bickering continued. They could lift a car easily, sure, but I could lift three. I mean... I didn't *know* that to be true, but I felt the brute strength vibrating through me easily enough. Maybe I could've even lifted four or five.

"Allow us entry, please," Jax said to the skinny guard. The poor fella truly looked like Barney Fife.

He furrowed his brow, fighting the compulsion. Some people were naturally adept at keeping their minds clear of influence. "Why would you want to come in on a random Sunday night? We're open all week."

Jax leaned in. "Let us in, then go on a two-hour nap in your car. And if there are cameras, turn them off."

Ol' Barney blinked a few times, then shuffled off to do as he'd been compelled to do.

I grinned at Jax. "I need to try my compulsion out now that I'm *all-powerful*," I said as we walked in. "I bet I'm better at it now."

Kendra, who'd tagged along, looked at me, eyebrows tilted in and eyes narrow and full of confusion. "What are we doing here? Isn't this the place where you bring old metal to get paid for it?"

Jax glanced at her and nodded. "Yes, we need Hailey to work out how strong she is."

Yessss. Excellent. I rubbed my hands together. "This is going to be amazing." Last night, I'd thrown the football almost a mile. Jax had beat it to its destination with me hot on its trail, and he'd made a one-handed grab that any pro-baller would've been happy to claim. Today, it looked like we were in for some sort of new training method that involved beat-up jalopies and dented fenders.

I waited for him to lay out his plan and tell me what he wanted, but instead, he picked up a motorcycle and threw it at me. A motorcycle.

With a screech I caught it—easily, I might add—and sent it back with a throw that went over his head. Jax vaulted into the air and didn't catch it, but pushed it, sort of, and it sailed straight for Kendra.

She'd wandered from the safety zone we'd established and was standing, looking around absently, near a pile of cars. If the bike hit the pile, they would topple, and the bike would fall, and Kendra would end up on the bottom of all of it.

Time seemed to slow in my vampire brain. I had only a sliver of a second to decide what to do, how to stop my friend from getting squished like a pancake or at best maimed by a half-broken two-wheeler.

I could've run, but there were no guarantees I'd overcome the impediments in the path and save her. And Jax was further than I was with more stuff in his way.

The whole terrible thing flashed through my mind like a movie.

The bike crashing into the cars.

The cars falling forward.

Kendra flailing, seeing death coming for her. I visualized all of it, and none of it ended well.

This couldn't happen. Something inside my mind snapped. A scream bubbled out of me. My fear and rage exploded from me and then...the motorcycle froze in midair, suspended about ten feet above the ground.

Kendra looked up with a slack jaw, then darted back toward the perimeter we'd set up as a safety zone, but when the bike stayed suspended, she stopped to look at me like I'd just announced my candidacy for president of the United States. A job, I might add, I'd be terrible at, although Jax might be awesome.

Jax stood stock still and stared up at the motorcycle, his neck bent, and craning. Everyone else shuffled forward from where they'd been playing to look.

"Holy Harley Davidson." Kendra walked in a slow circle beneath the bike, her head tilted up. "How did you...?" She glanced at me then back to the bike like she was waiting for the moment the magic wore off. Backing up a few more feet, she spread her hands out and mouthed wordlessly.

A thick line of magic ran from me to the bike, though where it'd come from and how it'd gotten there, I couldn't say. "I have no idea," I whispered.

It was a mystery or a miracle or whatever it was, it'd saved Kendra from going splat. Or being splatted. I didn't know if the terminology mattered as much as the act I prevented, but as Jax pulled her to safety beside me, the magic began to weaken. When she was fully out of danger, the turmoil inside me lessened, the magic dissipated, and the bike came down. Gently. Like I'd pulled it down with my mind. Nice and easy.

But I hadn't let it down. I'd just been relieved. The fear had lessened, and the panic had gone with it.

"Wow." I swallowed the lump in my throat. "That was…"

Jax looked at Grim and Nash, then at Paige and Ransom. Luke bounced up and down on the balls of his feet with his hands clasped near his mouth. He was ecstatic. This was a marvel, and no one seemed to know how it happened, only that it did.

"She can manipulate metal." Nash looked at me with his mouth hanging open. "I don't know of any other vampire who can do that."

Jax nodded and looked at me appraisingly. "Yeah. It's rare." A slow smile spread across his handsome face. "Special."

Before all this, the vampire fuss, I'd been sort of used to being special but for all the wrong reasons, for coloring outside of the lines and making mistakes no one else would've ever thought to make and doing it in grand enough fashion that everyone knew what I'd done. Either that or for being left at the altar. But this wasn't that. This was something big. This was actually *special*. And not in the my-mama-says-I-am sense.

"It's extraordinary." Paige looked at the bike, now standing on one wheel and a twisted front handlebar but standing.

I swallowed hard, which was another phantom pulse moment, and not nearly as fun as the others. This one was confusing. "Other vampires don't have this ability?" Jax shook his head, and I sighed. "Being a human freak wasn't enough for me. Now I'm a vampire freak, too."

Okay, okay. I was never a freak, *per se*. I didn't want to be one, though. Or call the council down on me for having powers they didn't think I should have—another opportunity for them to say I should not be allowed to be. That would probably be the next thing, knowing them.

Jax turned me toward him, took my shoulders in his hands, and rubbed my arms down to my elbows and back up. "No, Hails. Not a freak. You're something special, and these gifts don't come without a purpose."

All the pretty words in the world wouldn't undo the thoughts in my head. The proof was in front of us, standing on its bent frame. "What purpose could this possibly serve?" I motioned to the bike that finally fell over.

Kendra stepped forward. "You saved my life, best friend. I could've been killed." She wrapped her arms around me. "Leave it to you to look for the worst-case scenario."

I couldn't help it. I sighed again, even though the expulsion of air didn't come with actual wind from my lungs. It was only a token kind of gesture. "Well, let's try it again."

So, we did. Over and over. I wasn't able to recreate the hovering Harley even when Jax threw it toward Luke, but he would heal no matter what, so I didn't get the same panicked feeling.

It wasn't until we were walking through the lot that Jax jumped between the plates of the giant compressor that it happened again. I assumed it was the machine they used to flatten the cars when they were taking them wherever they took them once they were flat. I didn't need to know the logistics, but when the motor kicked on and the plates started to close a shield came down in front and Jax was trapped inside.

Trapped.

Inside.

I thought somehow, he would be able to move, but he stayed even as the plates moved closer and closer together and the sound of the hydraulic levels inside squealed and hissed. Panic burned up my throat. I couldn't do anything to get him out. He was going to literally be squished at any millisecond.

"Shit." My phantom heartbeat was set to explode my very real heart as I concentrated on those plates until they smoked, and the hydraulic levers stopped whooshing their power.

Jax shoved down the shield and stepped out. With a rush of relief, I let go of the magic so the compressor could work. It slammed the plates together hard enough that the ground shook beneath our feet.

It would've killed him. Vampire or not. There's no healing at that level of injury.

And with that, I knew the threshold for this particular bit of my power was unreasonable or reasonable depending on how I looked at it.

Fear.

Seeing those people I loved in danger was my trigger and with that terror, I could manipulate metal. I couldn't imagine another use for it, but surely there was a reason. And thankfully, it wasn't some crazy power like going invisible at the drop of a hat or walking through walls when I didn't mean to. This could potentially be helpful. Knowing I had it in reserve was enough. For now.

CHAPTER THIRTEEN

"Hey, girlie. Jordan has a skip for us to find and bring in." Bond Girls Recovery hadn't had a big score in a while, so I was excited even before she continued. "This one is substantial—a woman who embezzled money, a lot of money, from a client, then skipped her trial."

"I like it." I was a firm believer in no pain, no gain, but sometimes an easy day was nice, too. Embezzling ladies were generally pieces of cake.

"I'm sending the file to your email. Should be a breeze. She's about ninety pounds soaking wet."

I put my phone on speaker so I could open my email and look at the picture Cleo sent. She was right. The small woman looked young, innocent almost. Mousy blonde hair. Slight build. Claudia Wilcox.

"You in?" Cleo asked.

"You bet I am." Of course, I was in. I was dying to concentrate on something other than my vampireyness. Of course, being a vampire almost always helped us when we were out on a case. I wasn't denying that having speed no human skip could match and now the strength, too, weren't major perks, but lately, it seemed like that was all anyone cared about. What I could do. Who I was didn't seem as important anymore.

I wasn't going to go off on that tangent, though. That was me seeking something to complain about. Luke used to tell me I'd complain about winning the lottery.

He was probably right.

After a quick shower and a change into fitness attire that made running much more convenient than jeans, Paige and I picked up Kendra, then Cleo. Since she'd been injured—which was how I'd met her when I'd applied to be her caregiver—Cleo only liked to go along on the simple cases. Often, Kendra and I just stood back and watched while Cleo did the apprehensions on these little piddly skips. We hung close in case there was a safety issue, but otherwise, we didn't intervene.

Not that Cleo needed protection. Even post-injury and at her age, she was a badass. But she was human, and there were still council members swarming around. I worried, of course. No way was I letting her go out alone.

From the file—which Jordan had long since learned needed to include something personal of the skips, though I'd never asked how—we had a hair clip. Kendra used it for the location spell and within minutes, we had a location.

It wasn't anywhere close to where I thought we would be looking for an accountant. But Claudia Wilcox wasn't an accountant, apparently. If she was, she'd chosen an odd place to work out of. "Are we sure this is right?" I asked from the driver's seat.

Kendra nodded and tapped the file. "I double-checked in the car on the way over here. She's still here."

I stared up at the sign for the Boobie Trap and sighed. One of us was going to say it. I looked at Cleo, but she just grinned, so I shook my head and waited. Nope. It was gonna have to be me. "Never had a skip at a titty bar before," I drawled.

Kendra dissolved into giggles as Cleo horse laughed, then said, "Our ad says *anywhere, anytime*."

Today, we were going to prove it. "Let's do this." Climbing from the car, I walked to the leather-padded door and pulled it open, following Cleo and Kendra inside. A burly bouncer stood inside the door but only gave us the stink eye. He didn't even card us.

Um, insulting. Cleo and Kendra looked their ages, but I was a *vampire* for garlic's sake. I looked young.

Not under twenty-one young, at least not according to the beefcake who didn't card us.

Hmph.

It was like a whole other world inside the club. Lights strobed across three stages with women in various degrees of undress. One gyrated against a pole as men threw bills on stage. Another one had a sex toy! Holy crap, I didn't know they did that stuff in places like this. My goodness. The last stage had a couple of chicks making out. Music pounded and men and a few women sat at tables near the performers.

I'd never seen so many boobs and hoo-hoos exposed in one place before. Of course, I'd not spent a lot of time in strip clubs in my life.

I hadn't prepared myself for all the nips. They were everywhere. The servers, bartenders, women just sort of lounging around. So many perky pink-tipped tits. There was nowhere safe to land my gaze.

Cleo started walking the length of the floor, checking the chairs and the stages against the picture of our skip. As we followed her, Kendra gasped when a guy grabbed Cleo by the arm. Kendra pulled her taser from her bag—this wasn't the kind of place she would use magic, for fear of being seen—and was about to zap him in his protruding erection when Cleo gave him the old one-two, and down he went.

It wasn't three seconds later that a man with the distinct aura of a manager about him approached. Cleo marched up to him and showed him the picture of our skip. "Have you seen this woman?" she asked over the club's pulsing music.

This guy was a taller, skinnier version of a turtle, with hunched shoulders, a mostly bald head, and beady eyes behind big glasses. He looked at us appraisingly. "Auditions are on Tuesdays from three to seven for the new mature night. But we're only doing monthly runs for Old Maid Mondays until we see how popular it is."

I looked at Kendra and widened my eyes because clearly, he was talking to Cleo and not to us. She said, "No, thank you. We're here looking for this woman." She shoved the picture under his nose and waved it a bit. He studied it for a moment.

When he looked up, he pushed the picture back. "That could be Penny. She wears more makeup now and her hair's different, but I think it's her."

Cleo nodded. "Great. Where is this Penny?"

The turtle looked at her and grinned. "She's on next. You can talk to her after." He nodded as if he'd just made an important executive decision. Probably in his mind, he did. "Drinks are on the house for you tonight." As he walked around Cleo, he looked her up and down then leaned in, but because the music was loud, he spoke at a heightened volume. "And if you change your mind, see me on Tuesday." With that, he winked and walked away.

Cleo huffed out a breath, but her cheeks flushed, and she tried not to smile but failed miserably as a mischievous grin spread across her face. "Like I could do that." She nodded to the stage where a stripper was hanging upside down from the pole. Remarkably, the exposed ta-tas of the dancer didn't seem to be affected by gravity and hadn't moved.

We waited near the bar for Penny's turn, then clapped like we belonged here when the DJ announced her. "Ladies and gentlemen, please welcome to the main stage Miss Penny Tration!" His voice boomed over the speakers and there was a smattering of applause. One of the other dancers rolled her eyes and stopped to stare as Penny strutted out. Bless her heart, she tripped on the step going up. I sighed in relief when she caught herself, but then she stumbled, diving head-first into the pole.

The room recoiled, and several people gasped. Not a small number of the patrons laughed, but Penny recovered quickly, pasted on a smile, and started her dance.

Leaning toward Kendra, I nudged her with my elbow. "I can't tell if she's our skip or not."

Kendra shook her head and shrugged. "Same." She didn't have to speak loudly. I heard her by focusing my hearing, something I'd been practicing in Catch and Release. It served me well here.

Focusing on the dancer again, I tried to confirm if she was our mark. Her hair in the picture was semi-blonde, and she wasn't wearing makeup in it. This woman was the extreme and exact opposite. As in, if there was any makeup left in the dressing room that she hadn't spackled onto her face, I would've been surprised.

I focused on the show and watched her walk to the edge where a man was waving a dollar bill. She squatted in front of him, and he shoved the bill into her G-string before she stood then froze before grabbing her lower back and limping toward the pole. Ouch.

When Penny swung around the pole, hanging on with one arm and pulling off her bra top with the other, she twirled, slipped and slung a leg out. Her bra top went sailing and landed on Cleo's head, to our utter delight. And then, because there hadn't been a broken bone or any other injury yet, the stripper hitched her legs around the pole, used her thighs and calves to hang upside down, and promptly slid headfirst toward the ground.

The crowd gasped. Well, everyone except Paige. She usually stayed outside stationed by a door when we went in, in case a slip made it past us. That was where we'd left her.

"When did you come in here?" I asked. But Paige ignored me, staring at the stage like the sunshine itself was dancing instead of this clumsy woman.

"She has nice boobs." Kendra nudged me. "But, man, she's a *horrible* dancer."

The woman on the stage had forsaken trying to climb the pole and instead was dancing—maybe she was trying to do the robot?—near the chair of the guy who'd given her the only dollar in her G-string. That fella had long since left. Completely ignoring us as we gawped at her, Paige walked forward and sat right at the stage.

I followed, insanely curious about Paige's suddenly erratic behavior. "What are you doing?"

"We can't put her in jail." Paige couldn't take her eyes off of this woman and if this was just some passing attraction, it would have to pass. We hadn't had a really good catch in a while and this one was worth some serious moolah.

"Why not?" I asked, seriously suspicious I knew what she was going to say.

"She's my..." Paige stood up and clapped as Claudia finished dancing. Up close, looking under the layers of makeup, there was no doubt this was the woman in the picture. Paige smiled at her and continued clapping. "She's my fated mate."

Because of *course*, she was.

CHAPTER FOURTEEN

We all stared at Paige. Fated mate. Yup. We'd heard that one before. At least, Kendra and I had because Jax and I were fated mates. Cleo might've heard whispers about it, but it didn't matter. The meaning was clear, even to someone who didn't know much about vampires.

"Paige..." I said in a warning tone. It made the most sense that I would be the one who argued the point with her. The likelihood of Paige finding her fated mate in a titty bar...*and* that it would be one of our skips? That was far too much of a coincidence.

Kendra was forming a line right behind me, eager to talk to Paige. "Maybe she's innocent. The least we can do is talk to her first." I tilted my head and sighed, which was one of my habits that Paige wasn't a fan of.

She cocked an eyebrow. "I can compel her to tell the truth."

Cleo held up a finger. "This is a moot point. She's a skip. It doesn't matter if she's innocent. Jordan put up the money to get her out of the pokey and if she doesn't show up—and news flash, she didn't—he loses that cash. Also, we don't get paid."

Kendra stared at Cleo's lips. Paige and I could hear her fine over the noise, but she wasn't shouting, so Kendra's witch ears couldn't keep up. Kendra just shook her head and shrugged.

Cleo was the voice of reason, and she'd heard all the innocent stories before from the hundreds of skips she'd caught and brought in before I ever met her.

Despite that, I couldn't deny what I saw in Paige's eyes. Everyone looked to me to decide.

I didn't know why it fell to me, but I sighed again. Maybe because I was Jax's mate, and he was the leader. Our business was supposed to be a partnership, though. "Okay. We can talk to her first."

As a group, we walked the hallway to the dressing rooms. The *empty* freaking dressing rooms. "She's not here," Kendra said dully.

Obviously.

"Shit!" Paige took off running.

I ran beside her and from behind us, Kendra called, "Hey, slow down! I don't have superpowers!" Not to mention Cleo was barely walking upright. Okay, she was doing great, but she was still just a few months out from a gunshot.

Right now, though, we had a skip to trace, and I was tracing her. Or rather, I was chasing the vampire who was tracking her. We ran down a hallway to a private lounge and tried not to look.

Listen, I really did try. But there weren't just hoo-hoos and tatas on display back there. A fair share of weiners were out for show and tell. And a couple of them were impressively large.

I was by no means a prude. A little spank and tickle was never out of bounds, but I didn't want to do it in public, and I damn sure didn't want to do it with a stranger, especially now that I was bonded.

To each their own. There wasn't time to obsess. We burst out of the back door and into the parking lot. "Dammit!" Paige cursed again. "I can't smell her anymore." Her voice was higher pitched than normal and borderline frantic.

Whoa. Could this really be Paige's fated mate?

Kendra barged through the door and laid a calming hand on Paige's shoulder. "It's okay. I tracked her once, I can do it again." Kendra's presence soothed, and I wondered if it had something to do with being a witch or if she was just that kind of person. Didn't matter, I was just glad she did it.

Kendra pulled out her map and Claudia's hair clip and tried to pin down the location right then, but nothing happened. "She's still on the move. We have to wait until she stops, then I'll find her." This she said more to Paige than to me or Cleo, and I understood. Jax was my fated mate, my other half, and I knew exactly where he was at right now, and I still felt off being away from him. If Claudia was Paige's, then at the least my friend's skin was crawling with the separation. And her emotions had to be going nuts.

"Paige," I asked as we walked to the car. "I hope we're close enough that I can ask this question without it being offensive."

She stopped short and whirled. "What?" The suspicion in her tone was heavy, but I just had to ask.

"Are you even gay?" I wrinkled my brow and tried to look sympathetic, rather than curious.

She mouthed at me for a few seconds. "No." Whirling, Paige marched toward the car, then stopped again. "I mean, I wasn't."

I hurried forward and put my hand on her shoulder. "You don't have to label anything. Have you heard of same-sex fated mates?"

She looked at me a little bit wild-eyed and shook her head. "Never."

"First time for everything," Cleo chirped. "You just be who you are, and it will all be fine."

Paige nodded as we got in the car. Poor thing. She looked totally shell-shocked.

I drove us to the coffee shop nearest the strip club. It was kind of funny, but no one stared when we went straight to a booth and spread our maps and scrying tools. Not even when Kendra spouted some Latin and cast a spell. Then again, the place was empty except for employees.

Of all the things I missed after becoming a vampire, coffee was a big one. I used to love lattes and frappes and espresso, cappuccinos, anything caffeinated and able to be flavored by milk and whipping cream. I still loved the smell, though, and this place was one of my ideas of heaven. I *could* still drink it, especially if I laced it with blood, but it always made me a little queasy, so I refrained.

Cleo came back to the table with a caramel frappe for herself and a cappuccino for Kendra. Paige and I could stop at Catch & Release for a sip after I dropped off Cleo and Kendra.

Kendra hadn't been able to locate Claudia yet and so we waited quietly, each of us eyeballing the still shocked Paige in turn.

Kendra tried every few minutes until finally, "Aha!"

Paige lifted her head and looked at Kendra with the widest eyes I'd ever seen on her. "Did you find her?"

Kendra pointed to the map. "Right there." I couldn't see the exact location, but Kendra knew and that was enough for me.

We headed deeper into the city, to a high rise of luxury apartments. I made pretty good money at this job, and there was no way I could afford such fancy digs. This ritzy place had a marble foyer, pillars next to arches that led to elevators, a doorman, and terrazzo-tiled floors.

It was elegant and beautiful and reeked of expense. Claudia was either independently wealthy or she actually was guilty of embezzlement.

As if she could read my mind—and I wasn't sure how strong a vibe I was putting out—Paige shot me a glare. "We're getting her story first."

I'd agreed, so I nodded, holding up my hands in surrender. Kendra, who'd been parking the car, joined us in the lobby and I compelled the doorman —a success I would celebrate with Jax later—to tell us the exact apartment Claudia was in.

"There is no Claudia in the building."

I looked at Paige. If our skip was here, she was using an assumed name. Maybe *because* she was a skip.

She had to know the cops would be out looking for her.

Or maybe because she wanted to throw anyone who was searching for her off the trail. Obviously. I felt a little like Sherlock Holmes having all these deductive thoughts.

"I smell her." Paige leaned closer to the doorman and sniffed then moved back and started sniffing the air, every inhale longer and louder than the last. "This way." She pushed the button to the elevator. "She was in here."

If she was in the building, of course, she was. When we were inside the elevator, Paige bent and started sniffing the buttons one by one. I watched, knowing she was looking for the skip's scent, but Cleo stared wide-eyed.

"What in holy hell is Lady Dracula doing?" Her hissed whisper wasn't quiet enough for Paige not to hear but she ignored it anyway while I chuckled.

I glanced at Cleo then watched Paige continue using her nose to trace Claudia's scent across the many buttons. "She's investigating. It's a new method."

"She looks like an old basset hound I had back in Louisiana." Cleo shook her head. "Dumbest damned dog in canine history, but he could sniff out a cheating ex-boyfriend from under nine out of ten porches in the bayou." She'd been a PI once upon a time, too. I wanted to hear her stories.

"She's on fourteen." Paige pushed the button to thirteen so we could get off there and take the stairs up the last flight. Scope the exits and guard them before we tried knocking. This was old hat for us at this point.

Once we checked that there was only one elevator and one set of stairs, I left Kendra and Cleo guarding them while Paige and I used her fabulous sense of smell, which was heightened because she was sniffing her *mate*, to find the right door.

She parked us in front of 1414 and lifted her hand to knock.

CHAPTER FIFTEEN

Paige knocked on the door as I covered the peephole with a finger. Claudia, AKA Penny Tration, opened the door. A dumb move. She didn't even ask who was there. I took advantage of her naivety and muscled my way in. Paige walked in as though she'd been invited and shut the door behind her. Gently. Almost as if she was afraid a loud noise would spook Claudia more than she already was.

Claudia was prettier in person but still had on enough cosmetics to gussy up the four of us and have enough left over to do a clown's face for the circus. Good grief. Talk about the opposite of Paige.

I glanced at my friend, waiting for her to compel Claudia to tell the truth, but she couldn't or wouldn't speak past the goofy grin on her face.

"How did you find me?" Claudia sighed and plopped down on an expensive leather sofa.

"Magic." I wasn't being facetious but hardly anyone ever believed me. "Why'd you run?"

"I'm wanted. I figured you were from the bond agency ." Her soft voice was almost reverent as she stared at Paige. When she turned to me, she wrinkled her brow. "Is she okay?"

"Concussion." I nodded. "Hit her head when she was chasing you." A little guilt on our side never hurt.

"Look, I know how it looks when someone runs, but I'm innocent." Claudia held up her hands and backed up.

"Sure." I wasn't disbelieving. I just didn't buy it. Everyone said they were innocent.

She sighed and repositioned her robe from the club, belted but gaping at the top. I nudged Paige who still hadn't stopped staring.

Claudia didn't notice, because she'd leaned over and buried her head in her hands. "I swear to you. I didn't do this."

"Where'd you get the money for this place?" The view alone was worth six grand a month, not to mention the can lights, the fireplace, the built-ins. This place was a palace.

"It belongs to a former client. He's in Paris right now." She sniffed and dabbed at her eyes with a tissue. "I shouldn't be here. He doesn't know. It's against the law, but I didn't have anywhere to go." She shook her head and stared hard at me. "I swear this is the only illegal thing I've done, staying here. The rest of it, I'm being framed for. And this is the only way I can see my daughter. She tells her father that she's staying with a friend." The words tumbled out of her without her taking many pauses to breathe.

"Tell me how you got framed." I wasn't trying to compel her yet. I was just asking questions because I'd promised Paige.

"Well, I've been accused of skimming money from my clients' accounts." She snarled her lip in disgust.

Paige still stared at Claudia mutely. "How many?" I asked. Not that it mattered. Even one was one felony too many. Worse, she'd still promised to appear and failed to do so. Jordan would have our heads if we let her go, but I still settled in to listen. And by settled in, I mean I crossed my arms and tapped my foot while Paige ogled her.

"*All* of the accounts my ex-husband and I worked on, I think. Or most, anyway. But it wasn't me. It had to be him. There isn't anyone else who could've done it." Her face crinkled and tears flowed down her cheeks. "That's why I skipped my bond. I have to prove it wasn't me."

Paige pulled me to the side. "We have to help her."

Oh, finally she spoke.

"Jordan—"

Paige quickly cut me off. "You have saved that guy *so* much money, and he knows it. He can give us this one, at least until we find out if it's the ex-husband." Paige was already convinced. Her eyes said so. "I can't compel her."

That seemed silly. "Why not? You said—"

"She's my *mate*. A vampire can't compel her mate." This was information I already knew because Jax had tried once and failed to compel me. I'd forgotten. Paige looked over my shoulder at Claudia and swallowed audibly. "You'll have to do it."

"Fine." I sighed, on purpose this time. Then, I concentrated on Claudia, who repeated her story as I urged her to be honest.

When she finished, I nodded. "Fine. But we are doing this by the book. Come back with us, let us put you back in the system. I'll get Jordan to redo your bond. That'll give us a little while to get the information against your husband."

She nodded with tears rolling down her cheeks. Paige sat beside her, looking incredibly tentative, which was very un-Paige. "We're going to help you." She patted Claudia's hand and let hers linger until Claudia looked up at her and smiled.

"Thank you," she whispered.

A few minutes later, we walked out into the hallway with Claudia dressed now, face scrubbed clean, wig left on a mannequin head in the bedroom. Kendra rushed forward. "What happened?" I filled her and Cleo in, then we all rode the elevator down.

Paige sat in the back with Claudia between her and Kendra as we rode to the police station. "After you're processed, we'll start looking for your ex-husband."

Claudia sniffled again. "He'll never tell the truth. Not so long as he can pin it on me. He'll get the house and our little girl. He'll get everything." Her voice cracked and she was on the verge of crying again.

"I have ways of convincing him." The menace in Paige's voice was indicative of how far she would go, but I would help her stem the anger so we could get evidence the courts could use to exonerate Claudia and put her rotten ex-husband in prison. It would be a win-win for all of us.

Paige stayed with Claudia as she was processed in. Since the officers were so used to seeing us, they were a little lenient about how long Paige was allowed to stay. We waited on her to come back out with Claudia, then Cleo called Jordan to process Claudia back out.

She told him it was a personal favor, so he complied. He'd had a thing for Cleo since he'd met her years ago. He hadn't acted on it, as far as I knew. I loved Cleo, but she and I weren't *that* close. I didn't want to ask her to kiss and tell.

While we waited for the paperwork, Paige sat in the lobby with a handcuffed Claudia and they chatted, laughing even. Paige was hardly ever so animated. Thank goodness she'd stopped being a shocked zombie, at least. I wasn't sure I'd ever heard her giggle, but she was now. What a change.

I was glad for her. She deserved happiness. What I didn't know was whether or not Claudia had realized yet that she was attracted to women. If she hadn't yet, it would be soon.

Every life needed a surprise… right?

CHAPTER SIXTEEN

Every day we didn't find Claudia's ex-husband was another day that Claudia had to spend in jail. The judge who'd presided over her arraignment had refused to let her bond out a second time since she'd jumped bail. So, she'd remained in county lockup, none too happy with me, but Paige went to visit every day and kept her posted. While she was there, she worked with her, asking questions so we knew what evidence we would need to get out of the prodigal ex-husband.

Today was our lucky day. Kendra and Cleo had spent the day staked out at Claudia's ex-husband's sister's house.

While I was still sleeping happily, I got a call. "The eagle has landed." Cleo's voice was nothing more than a whisper, and it was as if she was standing near whatever *eagle* she was talking about.

"What?" I might've only just woken up and might've not had any O-neg yet. I might need to add a little coffee to my drink tonight, despite the potential for queasiness. I peeked out the curtains by the bed. Was it even dark yet?

"Wake up and listen Hailey. The *eagle* has landed." When I didn't answer, because saying it a second time didn't make it any clearer, she raised her voice. "The husband, Blood-for-brains. The ex-husband is the eagle, and he's at his sister's house."

Yawning, I woke up enough to process. Oh. Now that made more sense. "Okay." The bastard had come back for the trial, which was supposed to start first thing Monday morning. "All right. I'm on my way."

I wasn't dressed in more than one of Jax's t-shirts and a pair of panties. No, check that. The panties hadn't made it through the night, er, day, because at some point we'd gotten frisky, and he'd torn them off. I went through so many panties that way.

After a world-record-fast shower, I slid into a pair of jeans and a shirt of my own, then tore out of there like I had Buffy the Vampire Slayer holding a stake behind me. By the time I arrived, Kendra was posted at the back gate of the sister's house and Cleo hid near the front porch. They'd violated every s*tay in the car until one of us got there* rules Paige and I had dictated, but I bit my tongue. I wasn't about to say anything while Cleo looked so damned fierce holding a can of mace in one hand and a .22 in the other.

"You sure it's him?" I asked. It was the only question of doubt I was going to allow myself.

She waved the gun toward the ground like a properly-trained gunslinger. "Yeah. Every so often he comes out onto the porch to smoke." She shuffled the gun and the mace to the same hand, and I ducked as she swung toward me, but her gun was still down, as she held out the wedding picture Claudia had given us. "It's him."

I nodded without looking at the picture. If Cleo said so, I believed her. All I had to do now was wait for him to come out for a cigarette, and I would grab him.

It only took about thirty minutes before he walked outside. I snatched him right off of the porch before he could even think to say, "What the hell?" Although, he did say it.

It wasn't easy, not because he was heavy, but because he was easily twice my size and it was awkward as frick, but I carried him to the van I'd borrowed from Jax, tossed him in the back, and climbed in after him. Cleo was in the front seat now, with Kendra beside her. Paige appeared at the back door, glowering. I'd texted her the location before I left the house.

"Glad you found the place," I said.

She nodded, then returned to glaring at Dave.

For a few seconds, before I spoke, I glared at him, then let my fangs drop. It was a parlor trick, mostly, but it was enough to scare him into squealing like a little girl at a scary movie.

"Lie to me and I'll drain you," I said in my scariest vampire growly voice. "Then I'll go inside." I didn't finish the threat because my moral code wouldn't let me. No way I'd drain his innocent sister. Pfft. Dave didn't need to know that.

He got the idea and nodded.

"Good. Now, tell me all about what you did." I hadn't even attempted to compel him yet.

He shuffled closer to the front seat and Kendra made a hissing sound. She didn't have fangs, but he squealed again. It took *all* of my restraint not to laugh.

I shook my head at her. "What are you doing?" I mouthed behind Dave's back. He was staring at Cleo now, no doubt wondering what she might do.

Kendra's smile was enough to make the laughter bubble over, though I kept it silent. "You always get to have all the fun," she said.

"You want to question him?" I held up my hands and scooted away from the jerk who was still whimpering like a child.

"No, you go ahead." She covered her mouth and turned around, laughing silently.

I rolled my eyes. This was hardly the time to let our egos get in the way. "You can have the next time."

Before I even managed to ask a question, Paige leaned into the van. "This is no joking matter. Get this guy to sing."

"Okay, I'll have it out of him in a minute." I looked at the almost-sobbing fool in front of me. "Listen, asshat, you tell me what you did to frame your ex-wife, and I'm going to let you walk out of here." Straight into the police station, but I didn't tell him that part.

"I don't know what you're talking about." I didn't know if the fear was an act or if this anger was, but his eyes flashed, and he shook his head. "My ex-wife stole the money."

"Mm. So you say." I wasn't getting the truth without using my wily vampire ways, so I stared into his eyes and concentrated. It took a couple of seconds, but he spilled the truth, telling us exactly how he'd taken the money and which banks he'd put it in. This stupid SOB had left himself a paper trail in a ledger on his laptop.

Wow. How had he gotten this far with framing his ex-wife?

For a second, I wondered if I could get him to go back inside to get it and bring it to me, but there were too many variables without showing my face to his sister and daughter. This was a case for the real police, and since he'd put the money in offshore accounts, probably the FBI.

Jax had friends, so I gave him a call with the information. We only had to wait about an hour before his FBI buddy showed up. They hauled the ex-husband in for us, and Paige drove Kendra to the jail to pick up Claudia, however long that took. Kendra knew all the legalese being a lawyer and all, and Paige wanted to be there to greet her mate. I drove Cleo home, then I hightailed it back to Jax. We snuggled on the sofa to watch a movie. We'd both put in a fine day's work. He on whatever his problem of the day had been with his kingdom, and me with Claudia. I couldn't help but be pleased with ourselves.

Right as the boat was bobbing up and down and Jack told Rose to take a deep breath when he told her to, someone knocked on the front door. I stood to answer because I wasn't a huge fan of Jax's habit of just shouting for guests to just, "Come in!"

Kendra rushed past me, hands swiping together as she walked. When she turned to look at me, she was almost bouncing up and down with excitement that made her eyes sparkle, too. "I hate contracts. Did I ever tell you that?" She had mentioned it once or twice, but she also said it made her a boatload of money and she wasn't interested in being poor. I understood that. I didn't get to say it though because she was still talking. "I have an idea. Actually, more than an idea. I made a decision."

I nodded. "Okay."

She motioned toward the back door. "I need to bounce it off of you and if you're going to tell me it's dumb I don't want anyone else to hear."

I would only tell her it was dumb if I thought it was something harmful. And I wouldn't use the word *dumb*. Probably. But I led her out the back door onto the patio to watch Grim and Nash on the back lawn, sparring, throwing each other down, laughing, and each proclaiming themselves the victor.

I laughed when Grim tossed Nash, then stood like Captain Morgan with his foot on Nash's chest for a second before Nash grabbed said foot and threw Grim backward.

They wrestled while Kendra and I watched. Finally, she turned to me. "I took Claudia's case."

I nodded. "All right."

"And I quit Johnson and Baker." The law firm where she worked, specializing in contract law.

"That's a big step." It was as close to reminding her of her giant paychecks as I was about to get. I wanted her to be happy, and if she thought she could do it without raking in the big bucks, I would be supportive. It was our thing. We supported each other.

She nodded. "Yeah." She was back to wringing her hands, so I laid mine over them to stop the frantic movements. She chuckled. "It's a lot of money to give up. I know that, but I make more money than I need between the day job *and* skip tracing with you." It was true that we were all doing pretty okay with skip tracing. "This way I can finally use my law degree to help people." A second later, she turned to me. "*We* can help people."

"We?"

"If you can compel the clients I take on, pro bono, whenever needed, of course, then we can help people."

"And if they're guilty?"

"Then they're guilty. I won't take their case. But have you ever wondered how many of the people we hunt down skip because they're innocent and they're afraid?" She sighed. "I think about it all the time. Claudia, for example. Look at her. She could be doing years in prison right now if she hadn't run, and we hadn't found her ex-husband."

She didn't have to sell me on the idea. I liked it. "Ken, if you want to join the circus and need my help, I'm going to put on the makeup and get there with you."

She pulled me into a hug that would've crushed me, had I not been of superior vampire stock. "You're the best friend I've ever had."

"Ditto." I yawned as we pulled apart and she watched Grim throw Nash over his shoulder and run in a circle. Grim, not to be outdone, stiffened his body and slid out of Nash's hold. Then Grim used his momentum to pull Nash down, turned him face first, and rubbed his face in the dirt. These two were like the Abbott and Costello of vampire wrestling.

I turned and went back into the house and Kendra followed. "I know you're tired, but can we talk more tonight?" she asked.

"Of course." I hugged her again then walked her to the door. When she was gone, I turned. Jax was already asleep on the sofa. I stared at him for a few seconds. He was a beautiful man. And there wasn't much I wouldn't do to be with him.

CHAPTER SEVENTEEN

WE'D JUST WALKED IN THE HOUSE FROM CATCH and Release when Jax's phone rang. He answered it on speaker. "This is Jax Parsons."

"Jax?" The woman on the other end sounded tentative. "This is Ava Harper. I used to own the house across the street?"

I raised my eyebrows. I would've thought she'd be calling me rather than Jax, but I was deeply curious as to why she'd rung us at all. Ava was half witch, half necromancer, and I'd bought my house from her several months ago. She was a sweet woman and had kept in touch. She knew about Jax being a vampire, so I'd updated her all about my vampiric journey.

"Hello, Ava," Jax said. "I've got Hailey here with me."

"Oh, hey, Hailey," she said warmly. "How are you?"

After we exchanged pleasantries, Ava got down to business. "The long and short of it is, your vampire council tried to have me killed."

"What?" I gasped. How in the world had they done that? I didn't have to ask or wait for an answer.

"Trying to keep the story brief, they found a Fae who wanted power. They worked out a deal with him to kill me, I guess because they figure I'm too powerful to keep alive."

"Geez, Ava, I'm so sorry." Jax sat on the couch and rubbed his forehead. "What can I do?"

"There's nothing now, not really. I'm not equipped to take on your council, not yet anyway, if ever. I just wanted you to know." She sighed. "The names I was given were Soran and Gretchen if they mean anything to you. I don't know if more were involved or if it was just those two."

Jax and I stared at each other. "Every time something crooked happens, it seems those two are behind it," I said. "We know who they are and have been dealing with our own version of similarr issues with those two."

"Well, that wasn't all. While I was in a magical sleep coma that almost killed me, Luci and Olivia freed my father from the vampire elder's prison. They are holding more necromancers." Ava's voice had an edge to it that I hadn't heard from her before. She sighed as if trying to calm herself. "I'm not sure what I'm doing about it yet. Anyway, I hope you're both doing well. I'll let you know if any other information comes to light, but I just figured someone in the, uh, *vampire* world needed to know this."

"You're right," Jax said. "And I'm the one who needed to know. It's fortuitous that we're friends." He paused for a second then said, "How's Wade?"

Ava sighed. "He's okay. We donate his blood most of the time, but here lately I think he's missing something. Well, my friends and family because my blood would turn him into an undead slave."

Jax had told me about the history between vampires and necromancers. The power that necros had was death magic and that allowed them to control the dead and things undead, like vamps. If Ava let Wade or any other vamp drink her blood that vampire would be tied to her and would be compelled to do anything and everything she said.

"If you want to send him to me for further training, he'd be most welcome. Grim and Nash would love to take him under their wings. They get bored guarding me since there's rarely much going on," Jax offered.

"That sounds wonderful," she said in a hopeful voice. "I'll discuss it with him."

We said goodbye, promising to keep in touch. When Jax hung up, he looked at me and shrugged. "What do you think?"

I knew what I wanted to happen, and I thought we had a plan of how to go about at least part of it, but I needed to know if her call changed anything for him. "So, what do we do?"

"We don't have evidence to accuse them of anything." He shook his head. "I wouldn't even know where to look."

Oh, he of little faith in the internet. I went to my long-ignored laptop and opened it, powered it on, and returned to sit beside him on the sofa. "The World Wide Web is your friend, old man." He was a couple of hundred years old, and though he still used technology, the old fogey had been burned once by something he'd read on Google, so he didn't trust the internet anymore.

I, on the other hand, loved the internet. I mostly used it on my phone, hence my ignored laptop, but this called for a bigger screen.

After grabbing my laptop, I typed Soran's name into the search bar, clicked enter, and in less than a second, I had eight thousand hits. Wow.

There was something wrong with the way in which the council behaved. And no, they hadn't violated the law or broken any rules, but only because they *were* the vampire law, and they created the rules. They tailored them to suit whatever their latest purpose. Like me being made, for example. Although, it had crossed my mind that they were targeting Jax more than me, but I didn't have anything to justify that feeling.

Too many vampires had enough of a grudge to make an uprising against them. At least, that was why I thought they didn't want any vamp made who didn't support their every idea. They voted, for heaven's sake. And in my case, Jax hadn't had time to plead a case, make an argument, justify anything before creating me at the spur of the moment. Neither had Ransom with Luke, not really. Who knew how his condition might've deteriorated at a moment's notice? His organs could've started shutting down at any time.

I scrolled through pictures first. It was one of my best research secrets. I used pictures to direct me to websites. Especially when I was looking for a person.

It didn't take more than fifteen minutes or so of looking, and there it was, like a giant neon sign. It was only a painting of Vlad, the Impaler. But I had news for all those folks who knew Vlad. He was Soran. Clearly, these men were the same. The exact same.

The painting was dated 1457 when he was Voivode of Wallachia, at the height of his cruel reign. I would've laughed at the porn star mustache, but this didn't feel much like a laughing moment. Later though, for sure.

I scrolled through more of his history. "Holy crap, this guy." He was a tyrant who'd employed torture and fear to keep his people loyal. Wow. Just reading about him gave me the willies. Soran's evil went back a *very* long time.

As I continued to scroll, skimming the information, another picture appeared, and I zoomed into the background. A lot could be said for what or who was found to be photobombing a freaking painting. The artist had to have had a purpose for who and what he put into it.

Boy, did I hit paydirt. "That's Gretchen." I pointed to the screen then turned it so Jax could see. "That is freaking Gretchen!"

He peered at the screen but shrugged. "How are we going to prove it? And what significance does it have?"

Well, wasn't that the million-dollar question? I had a brother who formerly owned an art gallery. Maybe he would have an idea. Or maybe he could get a copy of the painting. A good one. Hell, maybe even the real one. He had some magical sway over people, so I thought it would be quite possible.

And like thinking of him brought him to me, he walked in the front door of Jax's place, gushing as only he could. He clapped his hands together twice as if to get our attention like he didn't already have it. "Guess what? I just got a call from that detective at the precinct. He said they threw the book at Linda.

She's going to jail for her life, my life, your life, all the lives." Probably not, since Luke was prone to exaggeration, but I wasn't going to mention it while he was so happy, and it had been a while since I'd seen such glee from him.

We hugged and bounced and hugged some more. It was so good to have him back. I just hoped he was here to stay.

CHAPTER EIGHTEEN

I'd spent several hours each night between hunting down skips for nearly two weeks at the computer researching, trying to find dirt on Gretchen and Soran, and the only breaks I'd taken were to let Jax reward me for my diligence.

Heh. Reward. Wink, wink, nudge, nudge.

I couldn't even remember the last time I'd been to Catch and Release. Jax and crew had been bringing me bags of blood. They definitely didn't hit the spot the same way, but it was worth it. I was making real progress.

These ancestry sites were like treasure troves of junk on the council. I'd found an old journal someone had uploaded, supposedly fiction, about a man named Soran and a woman named Gretchen who'd led a witch hunt against necromancers. It was written in old English or some half English, half something else language that was hard to decipher without the proper tools, but the interwebz had them all.

Fiction, my left foot. This crap was true, disguised as a fantastical story.

It took me a few hours a day for several days to decipher it, but when I got it, I got it. I read passages to Jax while he played Xbox with Luke. "The gist is that Soran and Gretchen were instrumental in the witch hunts of Salem. Except they were going after more than regular witches. They were hunting necromancers. The recounting has been lauded as a fiction story someone told but knowing what we know about Gretchen and Soran, it's as non-fiction as it comes. This confirms what Ava told us about her father and the council holding necros as prisoners."

He paused with his controller in hand. "You're a genius, Hailey. We can search the official records and find out where they lived at that time. If it's anywhere near Salem, we've got them."

"I wouldn't say genius." Maybe I would. Or… "Expert researcher, maybe."

He grinned over his shoulder at me and set the controller down, removed his headset, and then turned to knee walk toward me. "I can say genius." His breath warmed the inside of my thigh a second before his lips pressed to the same spot.

I moved the laptop aside and let him advance in his quest. "I do like the way you say it."

"Ew," Luke said and disappeared.

"We should tell the others, probably." But he was already tugging my shorts off. The telling would have to wait.

I didn't get much research done for a while, but it was *very* worth it. I'd just put my shorts back on when Jax shouted, "Come in!" in response to a knock on the door. At some point, we were going to have to discuss that particular habit, but right now, we had to show Dominic what we'd found. Jax's master walked in, to our surprise.

"Dom," Jax said, surprised but not displeased. "What are you doing here?"

He chuckled and pulled me into a hug. "I've been traveling around the States since your bonding. When you called to tell me about Soran being in the paintings, I decided to head back this way and see what you found."

I handed him the laptop and showed him the photos of the journal, the files I'd saved, including the portrait of Vlad and the one with Gretchen in the background.

He nodded. "Interesting."

There was a lot more to say about it, but Dominic wasn't a chatty fella. "Right? So, I'm thinking that Gretchen and Soran have been following each other through history, causing trouble, wreaking havoc on the world in a way only they can." I sounded confident in the research because it all looked reputable. The painting had been curated and verified as authentic. The journal was marked fiction, but the details were too spot on to be less than the truthful recounting of events and players. I had every reason to be confident.

"It isn't a crime to stick close to the people you trust, and they obviously trust one another since they've stayed together so long." Dominic was a lovely man.

For him to be Jax's vampire father, for all intents and purposes, they looked nothing alike. Dominic was gorgeous but much stockier than Jax. He had a lot of muscles, just shy of the bulkiness of bodybuilders. But good looking or not, I wasn't entirely sure I could trust him. His loyalty was entirely to Jax. I supposed I would be safe so long as I was with Jax, which would be forever. He wouldn't hurt me knowing it would destroy Jax to lose me. At least, that's what he'd said.

But I couldn't figure out what he was doing here. I was about to open my mouth to ask when he shifted in his seat between Jax and me.

With a look from me to Jax, Dominic set the laptop aside and took my hand. "I came to tell you of a prophecy."

I lifted my head. "Did you just read my mind?" I'd *literally* been thinking it.

Dominic smiled and nodded his head toward Jax. "I did. And then I read his mind."

"Nice." Although it was anything but. I was going to have to work on keeping the walls up the way Jax had taught me. I shot him a slight scowl, but he shrugged, sheepish and adorable in his regret. He should be regretful. He needed to keep his dang walls up as well.

I looked back at Dominic. "Prophecy?"

He nodded and smiled but looked sad. "It is said that you, Hailey, are going to be the council's downfall."

Oh, sure. "The prophets know me by name?" I didn't bother trying to hide my eye roll. They were probably poking around in my mind anyway, so they already knew I'd thought *no freaking way*.

Hanging his head, Dominic laughed. "No, it didn't say your name. The prophecy said, *the changeling of my offspring, with the strength of steel, the speed of light, and the courage of a lion.*" He smiled and cocked his head at me. "Of course, I recognized you right away."

It was shameful to have my head turned by a little flattery, but I was that girl. "Charmer."

His grin spread wider. "There hasn't been a vampire born with your strength since Jaxon was made. Together, the two of you will be able to cause real trouble."

But it didn't make sense. These were vampires who'd lived for literally thousands of years. They were by no means stupid. "Why would the council push so hard for us to mate if the prophecy said whatever it says, and if they knew we would be so strong together?"

Dominic shook his head. "I don't know. I don't think they realized your full potential, and they wanted to control you, to keep you under their thumb. Now they realize they can't, and they want you dead." I needed more information, but I didn't even know where to ask. He continued. "They didn't realize until the party. Soran and Gretchen went back and started demanding the council push for more control."

I hadn't done anything at the party to show off my power. "How do they know I'm so strong?"

Dominic looked at me then Jax. "It radiates off you and the mating has only increased your power. I can feel it, and you can bet your pretty face the council felt it. As well as every visiting vampire in the place."

Oh, good. I gave off power vibes. Jax and I would be having a talk about why he hadn't told me. It also didn't explain why Dominic was just now telling us about this prophecy.

Unless maybe he was in on it, a decoy to make us feel like we had a friend. Jax frowned at me, and I wanted to put up a wall, but I didn't bother trying.

"Why didn't you tell us before?" I asked out loud.

Through all of this Jax had remained silent. I didn't blame him. Dominic was his maker, and he didn't often go up against Dominic. Luckily, the maker loyalty Jax felt for Dom, and I felt for Jax didn't extend to my feelings for Dominic. I could question him all day.

"Because I didn't know it. Soran and Gretchen only told the council about the prophecy to try to convince us to destroy the both of you." I couldn't get a good read on him, but his warning seemed solid since there wasn't a reason to tell us except to help us prepare to protect ourselves. "They called a virtual council meeting last night. Most of the council is traveling since we all came here for the party. We so rarely leave Milan, it's common for us to take advantage of traveling when we do get away."

We just had to figure out the best way to do this so that we could expose Gretchen and Soran for the problems they had turned out to be. At least we had Dominic here to help. Assuming I was correct, and he really did *want* to help.

CHAPTER NINETEEN

We went through ten solid days of trying to come up with a plan before I was too frustrated to sit and listen anymore. No matter how many minds we put together, we couldn't come up with a plan to take over the council or disband the one that was already in place, even. Not like we could attack them on their own turf. Although that was a battle I wouldn't have minded fighting. Even if we had to fight it alone. I'd been training and preparing. I was confident in what I could do. But Jax and Dominic weren't so sure.

So we tabled that idea. And no one we'd approached at the party or sent out feelers to after had gotten back to us. We were running low on trust. It was too hard to tell if they would run back to the council out of some misguided loyalty or maybe even the kind Soran used fear to build.

It seemed hopeless.

In late August, I was sleeping like a baby in the early hours of the morning when my cell phone rang. With all the power I'd gotten from Jax, I didn't sleep so deeply that I couldn't be roused anymore.

Unfortunately.

"'Lo?" I croaked into the phone.

"Oh, Hailey, I'm so sorry. I didn't think about it being late morning and you most likely sound asleep."

It was Ava. The necromancer who used to own my house. She'd become a friend of sorts. No doubt if she didn't live all the way over in Maine, we might've become true friends. "It's okay," I whispered. "I'm just talking quietly so Jax doesn't wake up."

I glanced over at him as he cracked an eye. "I'm already awake," he said groggily.

"Sorry," she called through the line as Jax sat up, his hair sticking straight up on his head. "I can call back."

"No," I said. It was annoying to be woken up, but she wouldn't have called if it wasn't important. "What's going on?"

"Would it be possible for me to ask a humongous favor?" She paused. I sucked in a breath belatedly realizing she wanted me to answer.

"It depends on the favor, I suppose," I said, trying not to sound half asleep.

"I was hoping my mom and dad, Aunt Winnie, and Uncle Wade could come to stay for a week or two," she said, speaking quickly. "Uncle Wade could use some more training from Jax and that crew, but the rest of them are searching for bodies."

"Bodies?" I asked. That sure woke me up. I didn't need *more* drama. Not that I wouldn't help her if I could, but... bodies? "What do you mean bodies?"

"They are seeking bodies without souls to inhabit so they'll be back in living bodies. It sounds really icky, but they're being very careful to find people who are truly no longer in healthy bodies."

I sighed. "That could be Luke." It could've been him, anyway. Thank goodness he'd still been *in* there.

"What do you mean?" she asked.

"My brother was shot," I explained. "And we nearly lost him. I wondered before he was saved if maybe his soul had already moved on."

"Well, my father can sense if the soul is departed, or lingering, or still fully attached. And if the soul is fully departed, Mom and Winnie have a spell they can use to inhabit the body and no longer be ghouls in reincarnated, still-dead, magical bodies."

I chuckled and looked at Jax. Covering the phone with my hand, I asked, "Do you mind?"

"No, it's fine with me. I've never heard about this body thing they're talking about, but it sounds interesting."

Returning to the phone, I said, "Send them on. I'm interested to learn more about this. I wonder if a vampire's body can be inhabited."

"I never thought about it, but it'd be fun to try," she said with a snort. "And that's a subject I never in a million years imagined I'd want to explore more fully."

After a good laugh, we banged out the details and hung up. And then Jax and I went straight back to sleep.

IT WAS the end of August and about three weeks since Dominic dropped the prophecy bombshell on us, and we were no closer to getting more proof on Soran and Gretchen. Nor were we any closer to having a plan of attack, for want of a better phrase.

Since it had been a while since Jax and I made time to go out, we took a break from plotting and planning and researching to go to his club, like a couple, to dance, to be as normal as our abnormal selves could be.

Catch and Release was busy, a lot of vamps were out tonight for whatever reason—celebrating summer in Philly before fall weather snuck up on us in a few weeks, I suspected—the place was wall-to-wall bodies.

The club was two-story with an old gothic-style look with a black, red, and gold color scheme. There were tall, round tables with fancy bar stools at each one scattered around the dance floor in the center of the room. Booths and other casual living-room-style seating filled up the space along the walls. There were two bars, one at each end of the ground floor.

The second level had less seating than the first for a more private feel. Groups of high-back sofas that curved in half circles about the size of a loveseat framed by matching armchairs were randomly placed around the floor.

The upper floor also had two bars, as well as an area with pool tables and dartboards.

Jax and I had a booth table on the second floor and my hip brushed against his when I shifted closer to him.

"I've missed this." He smiled down at me and slid his arm along the back of the bench seat.

Before I could answer, Meredith Bird slid into the seat across from us. "Jaxon!" This was the leader of the Northeast United States vampires. And she was here after not being interested in anything we had to say at the barbecue. Her being here now didn't mean that she wanted to talk to us about what we wanted, but only meant *she* had something to say.

Jax held up a hand to call off Grim and Nash—the bouncers at the club and Jax's personal enforcers—who'd moved as soon as they saw her. Somehow, she'd managed to sneak past them, which was no easy feat. Then again, she was an area leader for a reason.

She'd traded her ridiculous US Flag dress for something of the little black dress variety—spaghetti straps, short skirt that showed off her long legs, low cut front. She'd dressed to impress.

There was a desperation to her gaze that I recognized. Not because I felt it now, but I'd seen it, *felt* it before. It made her voice shrill. "I need your help, Jax."

"My help?" He sat back and stared. "I came to you for help."

She nodded and the anguish deepened the lines on her face. "I know, but"—she leaned closer—"I turned a human."

Oh, yeah. Jax and I were well aware of the punishment for such a crime. Although it had worked out for us, the crime could've carried the punishment of death. Mine, specifically, if the council had been so inclined.

"Why did you turn the human?" Jax asked, though, it didn't actually matter. He would help her anyway because he was that guy and because it was another dig he could take at the council. Plus, having Meredith Bird owing Jax a favor would go a long way toward getting her region to help us take on the council.

"Evan has been my companion for years. Since he was very young. And he was beginning to age. I couldn't stand the thought of losing him." She sighed and swiped a hand through the air. "I turned him more than a hundred years ago, and I've worked hard to keep it a secret, but somehow that bastard Soran found out. And now they're going to kill Evan, unless..." Her voice didn't just die, it dead-ended on a look that said she had the weight of the world already on her shoulders.

It took a second for me to ask, "Unless what?"

She wasn't looking at Jax anymore. Wasn't looking at me either. She wouldn't meet either of our gazes and I got a bad feeling in my stomach.

It took a few seconds longer for her to answer. "Unless I kill Hailey, but Jax, I would never do that to you." She shook her head as vehement as anyone I'd ever seen. "I could never."

"And there's no guarantee they won't kill Evan anyway." It was my dainty little neck on the line—quite literally since she would likely have to cut it to kill me—and in case she was wavering, I needed her to think about all the reasons not to trust the council.

She nodded at me. "Yeah. I have no reason to think any of them are honorable."

"Me either." She was preaching to the choir. "How can we help?"

We both looked at Jax. He sat back again, shaking his head. "I think you need to play along like you're *playing along*. Tell them you're getting close to Hailey." I could see the merit in his idea. Making them think she was getting close to me allowed her time to work with us to plan and it allowed Jax to keep an eye on her in case the game changed, and I was once again being offered as tribute to save the council.

Super.

Meredith nodded.

"And tell them that you lied to me and told me that you're here to speak with me about expanding your territory." She nodded again. I honestly believed if I gave her a piece of paper and a pen, she would've been taking notes. "Tell them that Hailey is never left alone, so you don't have any choice but to make friends with her so you can get her out for a girls' night. Also, tell them if they hurt your progeny, you will tell me, and the jig will be up but that you need time."

I glanced at Jax. *Jig is up?* I cocked an eyebrow.

I speak my own language, woman.

"I'm worried about threatening them, though." Meredith's forehead wrinkled and her eyes narrowed. This was honest fear.

Jax nodded. "All right. Just ask them to please keep him safe. Explain that you need time, so I won't suspect your motives are anything less than pure, and then you think I'll relax her protection."

Meredith looked at me. "Do you have protection? We've all heard of your strength."

I didn't answer because there was no point in giving away anything, to her or to anyone else.

Jax smiled at her instead. "It doesn't matter. We just need the council to believe she does. And we need to buy some time so we can build our alliances."

Having Meredith's vampires was a good start. And if the others saw her allying with us, maybe they would too. We only needed time to find out.

Hurry on to Book 5, Dominating in the Midlife

LIFE AFTER MAGIC WORLD

Life After Magic World

Math After Magic

New in 2023: Middle-Grade Fiction Set in the Life After Magic world! Now your kids can read hilarious adventures as well. Or you can. We won't judge. <3

Witching After Forty

A Ghoulish Midlife

Cookies For Satan

I'm With Cupid

A Cursed Midlife

Birthday Blunder

A Girlfriend For Mr. Snoozerton

A Haunting Midlife

An Animated Midlife

Faery Odd Mother

A Killer Midlife

A Grave Midlife

A Powerful Midlife

A Wedded Midlife

An Inherited Midlife

A Fiendish Midlife

A Witching Babymoon (*A FREE Witching After Forty book*)

A Normal Midlife

A Grand Midlife

Fanged After Forty (Paranormal Women's Fiction)

Volume 1 (Books 1-3)

Volume 2 (Books 4-6)

Bitten in the Midlife

Staked in the Midlife

Masquerading in the Midlife

Bonded in the Midlife

Dominating in the Midlife

Wanted in the Midlife

Sleighing in the Midlife

Awakened in the Midlife

Ransomed in the Midlife

Hoarding in the Midlife

Hunting After Forty

Midlife Hotspots

Midlife Sight

Midlife Accomplice

Godmother Training Academy

With the Wand in the Library

Wears Valley Witches

Volume 1

Next of Twin

Twinnin' Ain't Easy

Keep Your Twin Up

Clash of Twins

Twin Eater

OTHER HILARIOUS FICTION
FROM L.A. AND LIA

Life After Magic World

Math After Magic

New in 2023: Middle-Grade Fiction Set in the Life After Magic world! Now your kids can read hilarious adventures as well. Or you can. We won't judge. <3

Witching After Forty

A Ghoulish Midlife

Cookies For Satan

I'm With Cupid

A Cursed Midlife

OTHER HILARIOUS FICTION FROM L.A. AND LIA

Birthday Blunder

A Girlfriend For Mr. Snoozerton

A Haunting Midlife

An Animated Midlife

Faery Odd Mother

A Killer Midlife

A Grave Midlife

A Powerful Midlife

A Wedded Midlife

An Inherited Midlife

A Fiendish Midlife

A Witching Babymoon (*A FREE Witching After Forty book*)

A Normal Midlife

A Grand Midlife

Fanged After Forty (Paranormal Women's Fiction)

Volume 1 (Books 1-3)

OTHER HILARIOUS FICTION FROM L.A. AND LIA

[Volume 2](Books 4-6)

[Bitten in the Midlife](...)

[Staked in the Midlife](...)

[Masquerading in the Midlife](...)

[Bonded in the Midlife](...)

[Dominating in the Midlife](...)

[Wanted in the Midlife](...)

[Sleighing in the Midlife](...)

[Awakened in the Midlife](...)

[Ransomed in the Midlife](...)

Hoarding in the Midlife

Hunting After Forty

[Midlife Hotspots](...)

[Midlife Sight](...)

[Midlife Accomplice](...)

Godmother Training Academy

OTHER HILARIOUS FICTION FROM L.A. AND LIA

With the Wand in the Library

Wears Valley Witches

Volume 1

Next of Twin

Twinnin' Ain't Easy

Keep Your Twin Up

Clash of Twins

Twin Eater

***

Packless in Seattle

The Midlife Prelude

The Midlife Shift

License to Midlife

Primetime of Life

COMPLETE SERIES

Series Boxed Set

OTHER HILARIOUS FICTION FROM L.A. AND LIA

Complete Series Volume 1

Complete Series Volume 2

Borrowed Time

Stolen Time

Just in Time

Hidden Time

Nick of Time

Howling Creek Paranormal Cozy Mysteries

Familiar Magic and a Dead Wolf

Magic Mishaps and Hidden Agendas

Magical Midlife in Mystic Hollow

(Paranormal Women's Fiction)

Karma's Spell

Karma's Shift

Karma's Spirit

Karma's Sense

OTHER HILARIOUS FICTION FROM L.A. AND LIA

Karma's Stake

Karma's Source

Karma's Spice

Cornellis Island Paranormal Cozy Mysteries

COMPLETE SERIES

An Otterly Secret Scheme

An Otterly Ridiculous Riddle

An Otterly Laughable Lie

Midlife Magic Dating Service

Monsters Matchmaking

Trying the Trickster

Vetting the Vampire

Testing the Troll

Bellarose Cat Cafe

Secret Witches

Suspicious Wizards

Scheming Warlocks

Sisterhood of the Stones

COMPLETE SERIES

Citrine Wishes

Sapphire Omens

Onyx Interruptions

Wears Valley Witches

Volume 1

Next of Twin

Twinnin' Ain't Easy

Keep Your Twin Up

Clash of Twins

Twin Eater

Shifting Into Midlife

COMPLETE SERIES

OTHER HILARIOUS FICTION FROM L.A. AND LIA

Pack Bunco Night

Alpha Males and Other Shift

The Cat's Meow

Midlife Mage

Complete Series

Complete Series Special Edition

Unfazed

Unbowed

Unsaid

Uncaged

An Immortal Midlife

COMPLETE SERIES

Series Boxed Set

Fatal Forty

Fighting Forty

Finishing Forty

OTHER HILARIOUS FICTION FROM L.A. AND LIA

Immortal West

COMPLETE SERIES

Undead

Hybrid

Fae

The Meowing Medium

COMPLETE SERIES

Series Boxed Set

Secrets of the Specter

Gifts of the Ghost

Pleas of the Poltergeist

An Unseen Midlife

COMPLETE SERIES

Bloom In Blood

Dance In Night

Bask In Magic

OTHER HILARIOUS FICTION FROM L.A. AND LIA

Surrender In Dreams

The Firehouse Feline

COMPLETE SERIES

Series Boxed Set

Feline the Heat

Feline the Flames

Feline the Burn

Feline the Pressure

ABOUT LIA DAVIS

Lia Davis is the USA Today bestselling author of more than forty books, including her fan favorite Shifter of Ashwood Falls Series.

A lifelong fan of magic, mystery, romance and adventure, Lia's novels feature compassionate alpha heroes and strong leading ladies, plenty of heat, and happily-ever-afters.

Lia makes her home in Northeast Florida where she battles hurricanes and humidity like one of her heroines.

When she's not writing, she loves to spend time with her family, travel, read, enjoy nature, and spoil her kitties.

She also loves to hear from her readers. Send her a note at lia@authorliadavis.com!

Follow Lia on Social Media

Website: http://www.authorliadavis.com/
Newsletter: http://www.subscribepage.com/authorliadavis.newsletter
Facebook author fan page: https://www.facebook.com/novelsbylia/
Facebook Fan Club: https://www.facebook.com/groups/LiaDavisFanClub/
Twitter: https://twitter.com/novelsbylia
Instagram: https://www.instagram.com/authorliadavis/
BookBub: https://www.bookbub.com/authors/lia-davis
Pinterest: http://www.pinterest.com/liadavis35/
Goodreads: http://www.goodreads.com/author/show/5829989.Lia_Davis

ABOUT L.A. BORUFF

L.A. (Lainie) Boruff lives in East Tennessee with her husband, three children, and an ever growing number of cats. She loves reading, watching TV, and procrastinating by browsing Facebook. L.A.'s passions include vampires, food, and listening to heavy metal music. She once won a Harry Potter trivia contest based on the books and lost one based on the movies. She has two bands on her bucket list that she still hasn't seen: AC/DC and Alice Cooper. Feel free to send tickets.

L.A.'s Facebook Group: https://www.facebook.com/groups/LABoruffCrew/
Follow L.A. on Bookbub if you like to know about

new releases but don't like to be spammed: https://www.bookbub.com/profile/l-a-boruff

Manufactured by Amazon.ca
Acheson, AB